Going Out With a Bang

"Well, any time I get an opportunity to kill a man I've wanted to rub out for years, it just makes me thankful all to hell, you know. Sweet Jesus, I just might have to visit a church later on today and offer up a prayer of thanks. Hell, I might even put somethin' in the plate to show my sincerity," said Coffin.

"No need for gunplay, boys," Longarm offered. "I didn't come here after any of you. Got no wants, warrants, or papers of any kind. So, why don't all you gents just mosey on off and don't bother to come back."

Willy Coffin's hand darted for the Remington pistol hanging in the single-loop, Mexican holster on his thick, double-row cartridge belt. The outlaw's fingers had barely stroked the cut-bone grips when Longarm touched off a single, thunderous, ear-splitting barrel of a .10-gauge buckshot. A tight group of well-aimed lead balls smacked the gunman in the chest. The lick sent him staggering backward in a cloud of spent black powder that rolled from the boardwalk like a high plains thunderhead spitting lightning.

Coffin's hurried, drunken, cross-eyed grab for his pistol resulted in a misplaced shot that blew a hole in the top of his own foot. The combined report from both weapons, fired in such close sequence and proximity, ricocheted off the glass windows of every storefront in town, sped down Main Street, and headed for Mexico.

TABOR EVANS

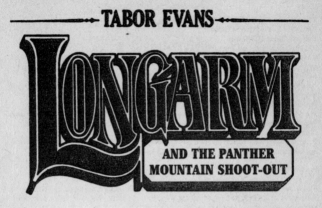

**AND THE PANTHER
MOUNTAIN SHOOT-OUT**

JOVE BOOKS, NEW YORK

THE BERKLEY PUBLISHING GROUP
Published by the Penguin Group
Penguin Group (USA) Inc.
375 Hudson Street, New York, New York 10014, USA
Penguin Group (Canada), 90 Eglinton Avenue East, Suite 700, Toronto, Ontario M4P 2Y3, Canada
(a division of Pearson Penguin Canada Inc.)
Penguin Books Ltd., 80 Strand, London WC2R 0RL, England
Penguin Group Ireland, 25 St. Stephen's Green, Dublin 2, Ireland (a division of Penguin Books Ltd.)
Penguin Group (Australia), 250 Camberwell Road, Camberwell, Victoria 3124, Australia
(a division of Pearson Australia Group Pty. Ltd.)
Penguin Books India Pvt. Ltd., 11 Community Centre, Panchsheel Park, New Delhi—110 017, India
Penguin Group (NZ), Cnr. Airborne and Rosedale Roads, Albany, Auckland 1310, New Zealand
(a division of Pearson New Zealand Ltd.)
Penguin Books (South Africa) (Pty.) Ltd., 24 Sturdee Avenue, Rosebank, Johannesburg 2196,
South Africa

Penguin Books Ltd., Registered Offices: 80 Strand, London WC2R 0RL, England

This is a work of fiction. Names, characters, places, and incidents either are the product of the author's imagination or are used fictitiously, and any resemblance to actual persons, living or dead, business establishments, events, or locales is entirely coincidental.

LONGARM AND THE PANTHER MOUNTAIN SHOOT-OUT

A Jove Book / published by arrangement with the author

PRINTING HISTORY
Jove edition / December 2006

ISBN: 0-515-14227-1

JOVE®
Jove Books are published by The Berkley Publishing Group,
a division of Penguin Group (USA) Inc.,
375 Hudson Street, New York, New York 10014.
JOVE is a registered trademark of Penguin Group (USA) Inc.
The "J" design is a trademark belonging to Penguin Group (USA) Inc.

PRINTED IN THE UNITED STATES OF AMERICA

10 9 8 7 6 5 4 3 2 1

Chapter 1

Deputy U.S. Marshal Custis Long, known by the nickname Longarm to friend and foe alike, snapped awake in his lumpy, run-down brass bed like someone had just cracked a bullwhip over his crotch. He blinked his way to full consciousness, scratched himself, stared hard at the grime-smudged ceiling overhead, then ran fingers through his shoulder-length hair and sniffed.

Approaching day crept into the windows of the rented corner room like a thief bent on stealing the darkness. The faintly musty smell of burning leaves drifted in through one of the open windows. Clouds of dust particles gently floated back and forth on slanted shafts of light. Dirt devils chased each other across the scruffy, worn carpet, then disappeared beneath the bed.

Long flicked his tongue across the back of his sleep-coated teeth; they felt and tasted vaguely like a saddle blanket after a week's use. He grimaced. A quick swish and swallow from a bottle of Maryland rye helped some, but not a hell of a lot.

His sleep-sodden gaze rubbered around the well-used residence and took in the sad, old-as-dirt examples of a dressing table, washstand, and badly discolored mirror. Piles of clothing, both male and female, littered the tattered, gray carpet that covered most of a stained, pockmarked, hardwood floor.

A strikingly beautiful, stark-naked female lay sleeping on her stomach beside him. She snored like a dull ripsaw chewing through thousand-year-old pine knots the size of wagon wheels. Bowtie-shaped, naturally red lips fluttered with each ragged, passing breath. The snoozing lady's waist-length, ebony-colored hair cascaded across one shoulder and dropped over the side of the bed. Her flawless and perfectly muscled back rose, fell, and rumbled in the rhythm of deep, comfortable, relaxed slumber.

Long's gaze skipped over his companion's silken locks, past her milky white, unblemished skin, and zeroed in on the kind of splendidly formed female ass that had the power to make any real man want to eat lunch off of it, then cuddle up with the wondrous thing draped over his head like a well-fitting, comfortable hat. He smiled at the thought of how a properly shaped woman's ass resembled an inverted heart, when studied from just the right angle.

After a mere five seconds of serious scrutiny of the subject at hand, his now-fully-awake lawdog felt about as agitated and randy as a Sonoran Desert–horned toad sitting in a red-hot camp skillet. Unbridled lechery reared its never-satisfied head between his legs in a rapid rush of intense, prickly heat, producing an angry, growing iron bar of rampant lust.

He turned onto his side and nestled the inflamed evidence of his yearning against the lady's shapely hip. Settled on one elbow, Long ran his fingertips in light circles from the nude woman's shoulders down, down, and down to the moist center of her being. By the time he reached the object of his unrelenting, penetrating efforts, she stirred, twitched, snorted, slapped at the invading fingers, then giggled.

"My God, Custis, you are an insistent scamp. Didn't you get enough last night? Thought for a while there you were about to wear the poor thing out. Sweet Jesus, I feel like I just traveled from Denver to San Francisco and back straddling a Butterfield stagecoach. Could be because of the ride you gave me."

He leaded forward, then breathed into her ear. "Hell, Tildy, I can't ever get enough of you, girl. You know that. Now, why don't you roll on over here and see if it's possible to do the big wiggle till our heads explode like a sack full of dynamite in a Leadville mine shaft. Helluva way to start off the day, don't you think?"

She hooted, flipped onto her back, eased her shapely legs apart, smiled enticingly, then sucked the index finger of one hand, while caressing a pair of pert, beautifully formed breasts with the other. Longarm pushed her hand aside, settled between her parted thighs, kissed her full on the mouth, and reveled in the pungent taste that reminded him of all the wondrously decadent things they'd done the night before.

Tildy's arms wrapped around his neck and forced his greedy mouth down to a pair of waiting, bullet-stiff nipples. She moaned as his eager and talented tongue flicked its way around each one. Somewhere outside the bedroom's open windows birds sang.

The take-no-prisoners warrior between Long's legs stiffened to the harder-than-a-cavalry-saber state. Love, lust, and the hunger-that-couldn't-be-denied propelled him forward.

The black-haired Tildy whimpered as he dipped into her wet, waiting sweetness. Like a pair of well-stoked locomotives gathering steam, the couple quickly pumped their primitive rhythm up to a boiler-busting pace. All the heat, effort, and invigorating carnality of exertion caused the lady's agile body to flush with a passionate, reddish sheen from the edges of her blood-engorged nipples to the top of her head. He almost laughed out loud when she brought her hips up as high as she could, bent her neck forward, and strained in an effort to see as much as possible of what was going on between her raised legs.

Matilda Potter worked hard, equaled, and sometimes surpassed, his every stroke, he'd give her that; but when she gasped, arched forward like a tightly strung bow, and watched, wide-eyed, as he thrust into her, Long held the rigid, muscle-quivering position of climax for almost a minute, then kissed her again, and finally rolled away.

A short time after completion of their impassioned, early-morning lovemaking the raven-haired beauty slipped from his side, dressed, and stood with one hand on the doorknob of his room. She ran a quick, appreciative gaze over his unclothed, exposed form. Her tongue moistened dry lips as she admired the particular portion of his muscular anatomy that kept her coming back for more every time he was in town.

"Will I see you again before the end of the week, Custis?"

He raised both arms above his head and posed in the rumpled bed in a way that insured she saw exactly what she wanted. "Should be able to see about as much of me as you want right now, girl."

"That's not what I meant, and you know it."

Long flashed a toothy grin and lifted one leg so the view became even more provocative. "I doubt it, Tildy. Would be great if we could get together sometime soon, but I've got a meeting with Marshal Billy Vail this morning. If the note he sent me is any indication of what's in store, I'll be on a train and gone pretty quick. Not sure how long it'll take before I'm back in the stable."

She snatched the door open, winked and said, "Too bad. This filly's got an itch only a randy stallion with equipment like yours can scratch. But you be sure and let me know as soon as you're ready for another romp. You'll do that, won't you?"

"Don't you worry, Tildy, darlin'. You'll be the first to know when I make it back to Denver. Promise."

"Well, that's good to hear, Custis, darlin'. 'Cause I can't wait to continue our efforts at trying to determine if it's possible to kill, or at the very least, maim ourselves making love, like a pair of wild West Texas mustangs, *big boy*. Next time out, I just might even bring along some Mexican spurs and my riding crop. With proper application of the whip, I'd be willing to bet I can urge you right along to even greater levels of performance than anything you've dreamed of so far."

"Nothing I'd like better," he said.

She flashed another winning smile, winked again, then quietly closed the door behind her.

Long closed his eyes and tried to visualize Tildy Potter dressed in nothing but a sombrero, high-heeled riding boots, Mexican spurs and slapping a riding crop across her palm. "Hot damn," he said to the empty room.

Chapter 2

About an hour after Tildy Potter's departure, according to the genuine Ingersoll railroader's watch he always carried in his vest pocket, Longarm stepped from the doorway of his Denver rooming house. The rented lodgings lay on the ramshackle, less than trendy side of Cherry Creek and he paused on the cinder pathway that led to the freshly-swept sandstone sidewalks of Colfax Avenue. He halted just long enough to pull a nickel cheroot from the inside pocket of his recently cleaned brown tweed suit jacket. The square-cut stogie was shoved between chapped lips. Without lighting the smoke, he turned on his heel, and, like a man on a mission, hoofed it for the Colfax Avenue Bridge and then turned east. The federal building, and the office of his boss, United States Marshal Billy Vail, was but a fifteen-minute walk.

Six feet four, lean as chewed rawhide, and muscled like a man half his age, the preoccupied lawman tipped his snuff-colored hat in the general direction of several attractive women he passed on the street. They, in turn, cast furtive, admiring glances his way. One *lady*, he noticed, unflinchingly stared below the buckle on his pistol belt at the juncture of his skintight, brown tweed britches. When he touched his hat brim and nodded to acknowledge her obvious interest, she blushed and huffed away.

Long noticed, but discounted, the men who crossed his single-minded path that morning. He observed the looks of unease on their faces as they detected his impatience, stepped aside, and tried their best not to make eye contact. He saw, but didn't care, that even the most casual, passing onlookers discreetly whispered behind cupped hands to their companions. And appeared to comment on his every stalking step. Their attention simply added to his growing irritation.

His purpose-driven stroll passed quickly in the pleasant nip of Colorado's crystalline, swirling, although odd smelling, fall air. The snow-covered peaks of the Rocky Mountains, some fifteen miles away, failed to soften the fit of annoyance he'd nursed since late the previous afternoon. A bout of exasperation and seething aggravation had stayed with him in spite of Tildy Potter's passionate and single-mindedly athletic attempts to aid and comfort him through the night.

Unfortunately, neither memories of stunning Tildy nor the picturesque landscape, nor the eddying waves and crackling crunch of paper-dry leaves he crushed beneath low-heeled boots served to divert his determined attention. The fuming vexation continued to bubble under an uncomfortable, starched-white collar. He flushed and pulled at the restraint around his neck for relief.

At Cherokee and Colfax, Long strode into the Denver federal building like a hungry wolf on the hunt, then pushed his way inside. He snatched the already mangled, unlit cheroot from between clenched teeth and thumped it into one of the federal building's numerous sand-filled ash cans. He grimly stomped his way through the crowded hallways and scurried up a marble staircase two steps at a time. The massive oak entrance of Billy Vail's nondescript government office sported an impressive sign in gold leaf lettering that proclaimed: UNITED STATES MARSHAL, FIRST DISTRICT COURT OF COLORADO.

When the outer door burst open like a clap of thunder rolling down the Rockies' front range, Vail's overworked administrative assistant jumped like someone had fired a pistol shot across the room. A hot-eyed Custis Long swept in with all the force of a scorching wind from somewhere west of Texas and south of Hell.

The by now red-faced, hard-working lawman threw an angry-eyed glance at the petrified clerk, and ran a tense finger under one side, then the other, of his drooping handle-bar moustache. "Don't you dare have nerve enough to ask me if I've got an appointment. No prior arrangement necessary this morning. I was sent for, goddammit."

Billy Vail's clerk nodded and said, "True enough, Deputy Long. I'm the one who penned the note that summoned you here this morning."

Long shook his head. "Hell, I figured as much, Henry. Is Billy in there?" he growled.

The marshal's assistant woodenly nodded and moved to stand, but never fully made it to his feet. He still hovered somewhere between sitting and a trembling squat when Long raised a forceful hand and motioned for him to keep his place.

"Don't trouble to announce me."

In what appeared an effort to regain some control of his tiny, administrative kingdom, the stunned clerk snatched gold-rimmed spectacles off and impatiently waved them toward the inner door. In a voice laden with a rapidly rising officiousness he snapped, "Why, yes. He's here and is expecting your arrival. Please go right in, Deputy Marshal Long."

The heavy, solid wood door to the chief marshal's lair stood partially open, but revealed nothing of what awaited inside. From somewhere behind the impressive portal, Long heard Billy Vail growl, "Come on in, Custis. Don't just stand out there in the lobby fuming."

It took only four steps to bring the irate deputy to a carpeted spot directly in front of a substantial, overburdened, mahogany desk decorated with mountains of leather-bound law books. There were also wanted posters, writs, court records, pistols, rifles, spurs, keys and foothills of other nondescript junk that had accumulated during years of law enforcement work.

Behind peaked fingers, Marshal Vail's moonlike face bobbled above his collar like a kid's gas-filled carnival balloon on a string. He threw his visitor a toothy grin, nodded and motioned toward the empty chair facing the desk.

Long huffily snatched a folded piece of note paper from his jacket pocket and waved it in Vail's face. "Dammit all, Billy, not two days ago you said I could have the whole, entire, and complete week off. I stood right in this very same spot and you, or somebody who looks a hell of a lot like you, told me what a damned fine job I'd done flushing Black Jack Cassidy out."

"True, Custis, every word of what you just said is absolutely true."

"Lord Almighty, you praised me from the rooftops like a Baptist tent revivalist on a soul-saving rip because I'd safely brought that stink-tailed skunk back for a dose of hemp-stretching justice. Talked about how Deputy

U.S. Marshal Custis Long deserved, and would have, a week's rest and well-deserved *recreation*. And you, better than anyone, know the kind of *relaxed amusement* I favor. Then, lo and behold, I get this note."

"Please, take a seat, Custis, before you have a stroke, bust a blood vessel in your fevered brain, have a heart attack, or something else equally death dealing happens to you."

"I don't want to sit down, Billy. As you well know, I can fume, fuss, and yell a hell of a lot better when I'm reared up on my hind legs like a pissed-off grizzly bear."

Vail tapped his still peaked fingers together and continued to maintain the blank, noncommittal stare of a man only mildly surprised at the blast of incensed vexation that now confronted him. "Well, now, look Custis, you surely know I meant what I said about the way you handled that brute Cassidy."

"I certainly hope so."

"The law needed him alive. And when you brought him back, he was still kicking. Slightly damaged, what with the broken arm, gunshot wound to the left buttock, crushed collar bone, and all. But he was at least breathing when you dragged him in—barely breathing I hasten to add, yet he did manage to occasionally suck down a ragged, raspy breath through all those broken teeth."

"Well, now, that's mighty big of you, Billy, given that the son of a bitch almost killed me at least twice—first when he attacked me in that Tucson livery stable with a bowie knife the size of a meat cleaver, and second when he came up swinging a set of red-hot horseshoe tongs. I'd venture to say his being alive makes him luckier than the guy who bought a cemetery and struck gold when he dug the first grave."

"Could you clarify one particular part of the initial confrontation for me?"

"Which part?"

"Exactly how on earth did ole Black Jack manage to get shot in the left buttock?"

Long ducked his head and wagged it back and forth like a tired dog. "Well," he said, "when the son of a bitch swung that set of horseshoe tongs at me, he kind of lost his balance, you know. Twirled around like a drunken ballet dancer and had his back to me when I, thank God, managed to get off my only shot."

Vail threw his head back and chuckled. "You shot him smack in the ass by accident?"

"Hell bells, Billy, I meant to kill the son of a bitch, but this double-action pistol I carry pulls a bit to the right. Not making any excuses, mind you, but I was in a bit of a hurry at the time. The way I've got it figured, he's damned lucky to be alive."

"Well, Doc Bryles fully agrees with you about that."

"Now I must admit that ole Black Jack won't be sitting like most folks for a spell, and I do regret that future trips to the shitter are gonna be something of a totally new experience for the man. But he's one lucky bastard none the less, because I aimed for his liver. And I would have hit it, if his big, lardy ass hadn't got in the way."

The chief marshal leaned forward, ran his fingers through wispy white hair, and then motioned toward the overstuffed leather chair again. "Come on, now, Custis. Calm down and have a seat. There's just something uncomfortable about having an employee looming over me like this that offends my overly important supervisor's sensibility."

"Already made it about as clear as a glass dinner bell I do not wish to sit, Billy."

Vail threw up his hands in defeat. "Fine. Suit yourself. Go ahead, be stubborn, and yell all you want, but when all the yelling's over, you've got to go to Panther Mountain, Texas, and damned quick.

Long's chin dropped to his chest. "Aw, Jesus, Billy."

"Early tomorrow morning would be a nice time to start. I've checked on the departure connections from here for you, arrival in El Paso, and such. Hell, I checked out your transport all the way to Fort Stockton. Got your rail passes all ready and waiting. Leave tomorrow morning and you can be there in an easy, relaxing two days. Hell, you should arrive all rested up and ready for a nice horseback jaunt of about fifty miles."

Vail's deputy moaned like a man who'd been struck with an ax and flopped into the tack-decorated leather chair. He crossed his legs, wearily removed his snuff-colored hat, and dropped it over the toe of one boot. "Can't you send someone else, Billy? If there's a godforsaken part of Texas, that's it. Actually, that's not exactly true. I don't think God has ever been to West Texas, so he couldn't very well forsake it. Could he? Then again there are rumors around that rattlesnakes get so lonely out there that they've been known to screw Gila monsters."

Vail leaned forward on his elbows like a man about to share a little known secret. "Please believe me, there isn't anyone else available at the moment," he said.

"Now, that's not exactly true. I just this very minute saw Joe Bell out in the hallway when I came in. Man looked about as bored as a frog in a skillet. Send him. Hell, Joe's from West Texas, born and raised somewhere over around Pecos. The man loves the bleak, depressing place. Most of his beady-eyed family are likely armadillos or some other kind of hardheaded rodents anyway. Put Joe Bell where a man can't see a tree for more than a hundred miles and he'll be happier than a flat-broke brush popper that just found out he's inherited a well-staffed, New Orleans whorehouse."

"Joe's on his way to Bisbee, Custis. Arizona's territorial governor requested some assistance with a festering cattle theft problem in the area south of the Dragoon Mountains. Needs us to help out with reports of several murders related to the rustling. Joe could well be gone for two months, maybe longer."

"Well, how about sending Elton Barber? Spotted that lazy slug loafing around on a bench out front as I was coming up the steps a few minutes ago. Man was asleep for crying out loud. Snoring so loud I heard him when I passed by."

Vail didn't hesitate with an answer. "Elton's leaving this afternoon for Thermopolis, Wyoming Territory, Longarm."

While the marshal's familiar use of Custis Long's nickname indicated a softening in the tone of their conversation, it didn't keep the irritable deputy from winching as he snapped, "And just what in the blue-eyed hell is the purpose of Elton's trip to Thermopolis?"

"Tyrone French's murder trial is about to finally get underway. Somebody's been making less than veiled threats against the life of Judge Henry Ewing. Can't have folks popping off about how they'd like to kill a federal judge, now can we?"

Longarm shook a weary head. As he fiddled with his hat, a hint of resignation crept into his voice. He said, "Tyrone French, huh? Hope the good folks of Thermopolis hang the wife-and-child–murdering son of a bitch. Somebody should have killed the man years ago. Could have been me a time or two, I suppose. Had him in my sights more than once, but he is one slippery bastard."

Marshal Vail stood, turned, and then pushed the heavy curtains covering the window behind his desk aside with one finger. He gazed out the dust-covered panes of thick glass for several seconds before he turned and said, "You've got far more important fish to fry, Longarm. Buster Byers, town marshal of Panther Mountain, is an old Texas Ranger acquaintance of mine. I received a wire from him late yesterday. Says he has Hangtown Harry Moon in custody and locked up in one of his jail cells."

Longarm sat straight up in his chair. "Hangtown Harry Moon? The greasy skunk that helped kill all those bank employees, and then murdered Judge Isaac Mumford?"

"Exactly."

"My God he's a bad one, Billy. About as bad as they come. Unless you start talking about his even more evil family."

"No doubt about it, he's a *real* bad one. If half the stories told about the man are true, ole Hangtown is one prolific and vicious thief and killer. Son of a bitch walked right into Judge Mumford's Santa Fe courtroom, bold as brass. Shot the hell out of poor ole Mumford because he justifiably sent Moon's cousin to the gallows for some of those bank killings you mentioned. Fired one bullet into Mumford's brain, then turned around and walked out like he owned the place. Got clean away. And you're right as rain when it comes to his immediate family, everything we know about them indicates his brothers are even worse."

"I must admit to having only met Judge Mumford a time or two, Billy. He appeared to be a gentleman of the first order. Do remember as how just about everyone around Santa Fe was mighty upset when Hangtown Harry blasted the hell out of the poor man?"

"Well, I knew Isaac Mumford and genuinely liked

him. Had dinner in his home a number of times. His wife and mine remained close friends, even after they left Denver and moved to live in New Mexico. About as fine a fellow as you'd ever want to know."

Longarm threw his head back, closed tired eyes, and pinched the bridge of his nose. Billy Vail was well on the way to beating him again, and he knew it. "Want me to leave tomorrow morning, huh? Already checked on the times and all? Got my rail passes ready, do you?"

Vail abandoned his spot by the window, rounded the heavy desk, and perched on its edge near his favorite deputy. "Yes to all questions, Custis. And while I know full well you completely understand the dangers involved in such an assignment, I feel it necessary to urge that you be extremely careful this time out."

"I'm always careful, Billy."

"That's true. But Harry Moon has a murderous family and friends under every rock between the Canadian border and the Rio Grande. Not to mention at least three near idiot brothers who are just as vicious and lethal."

"How long has Moon been incarcerated?" Longarm asked as he idly picked at flecks of invisible lint on his hat.

"Near as I can tell, Buster's had him locked up for about a week already. You must get down to Panther Mountain as quickly as possible and bring him back to Denver before some of his vicious Texas *compadres* or his half-witted family manage to find out what has befallen the man, break him out, and possibly kill Marshal Byers, and perhaps others, in the process."

Longarm came out of the heavy chair like an unfolding carpenter's rule, stood, stuffed the hat back on his head and said, "Billy, you realize, of course, that at least half a dozen of this city's neediest, most passionate young women will be denied my company and ardent at-

16

tentions as a result of this hastily arranged and irritating mission. Christ Almighty, what are young women to do if I can't see to their collective welfare?"

Vail smiled and, as both men moved toward the door, he patted his deputy on the back. "Custis, I swear I'll give you an entire week off as soon as you get back. Swear on the heads of my curly-haired children. Maybe I can even swing two."

"Save that self-serving blather for the newly hired and half-witted, Billy. I've heard that load of unmitigated horse fritters too many times in the past. I'll believe two weeks off when I'm laid up in one of New Orleans's finest hotels with the most beautiful woman in Louisiana strapped around me like my pistol belt."

The old friends stopped in the office doorway, as Marshal Vail shook Longarm's hand. "Henry has all the necessary legal papers ready for you. Now, while I know you don't have to be told a second time, do be careful out there amongst them. If Hangtown Harry gets a chance, he'll kill anyone who makes the mistake of getting in his way. As far as a man like ole Harry is concerned, you, me, and the rest of the good law-abiding folk in the world, are nothing more than a crop of puss-filled pimples waiting to be rendered out for squeeze."

"Well, like I just told you, Billy, no need to worry over my safety and well-being. It's gonna take more than a snake like Hangtown Harry Moon to send me to my Maker." He smiled, broke the handshake and started for the door.

Longarm paused briefly when Vail called out, "One other thing. As I mentioned before, Buster Byers is an acquaintance of mine from many, many years ago. However, I cannot in good conscience vouch for the man's grit, or honesty, now. So, should anything wayward occur, and you come to find yourself in need of assistance, seek out a gent who lives across Panther Creek and about halfway up the mountain. His name is Mica Hatchett. There's no doubt in my mind you can depend on Mica."

"How do you know this Hatchett fellow, Billy?"

"Why don't you ask him, if you two should meet. It's a long and boring story. Probably best he tell you the tale."

Longarm nodded and, as he passed the clerk's desk again, reached out and took the proffered envelope of legal paperwork, rail passes and other documents required for the trip and Hangtown Harry Moon's transfer to Denver. Without slowing so much as a half step, he waved good-bye with the thick package and vanished into the hallway.

Chapter 3

A boiling sun came up the morning after Longarm's
quarrelsome meeting with Billy Vail. The still mildly irri-
tated lawman tossed his Army surplus McClellan saddle
and bedroll onto the baggage car of the Denver & Rio
Grande western railroad's 6 A.M. passenger train headed
south to Trinidad, where he would switch over to the
Atchison, Topeka & Santa Fe line for the leg on to El
Paso. He stoked a cheroot and watched as a grunting,
sweat-drenched express agent moved the famed "ball
buster" off the floor and onto the lowest level of a set of
wooden shelves along the car's back wall.

When finished the agent turned, tipped his cap, and
said, "Pleased to help out, Marshal. No need to concern
yourself with your trappings any further. I'll make sure
they get transferred in El Paso so they'll be right there,
ready and waitin' when you terminate in Fort Stockton."

Longarm thanked the railroader and headed for the day
coach. He found a straight-backed less-than-comfortable
seat in the sparsely populated train car, covered his face
with his hat, and almost immediately dozed off.

Vivid reveries of Tildy Potter, and their recent night of

19

unbridled passion, brought a smile to Long's sleeping lips. And, on several occasions, visions of the randy girl's near perfect face shattered his peaceful slumber and brought him back to staring out the window until sleep took over again.

Longarm had made the same trip many times in the pursuit of evil men, but the impressive sight of the Rockies from his spot next to the window no longer held quite the interest of an uninterrupted, rocking nap. Not even the spectacular view offered by Raton Pass held any interest for the napping lawdog. He knew that without doubt, as in the past, the lengthy journey would prove boring and uneventful.

By the time he arrived in El Paso the late-afternoon temperature had gotten decidedly warmer. He stripped off his jacket and said to himself, "Jesus, it's hotter'n a two-puckered owl."

His rail connection headed southeast to Fort Stockton was running later than expected—much later. After a near torturous two-hour layover in an ovenlike station house, the dripping-hot lawman hoisted himself aboard another sparsely occupied coach.

He deliberately filled the empty rear-facing spot directly across from his seat with a pile of gear that consisted of saddlebags, rain slicker, rifle, and other paraphernalia. His effort was designed to take up as much room as possible in the hope of discouraging those who might invade the space as the steamy day wore on and more passengers came aboard.

Hours later, after stopping at almost every hole in the rail line's South Texas road bed, Longarm awoke from a clammy nap, when he felt the jolt of couplings as the still lightly peopled train began to slow. The first thing the drowsy lawman noticed, as he wiped at sleep-filled eyes, was an elderly Mexican farmer two seats down and across the aisle. Accompanied by a small child, the stoic peon held a nervous chicken on his lap. Must be their supper, he thought. The man, boy, and chicken appeared to be the lawman's only traveling companions.

Molten rays from a blistering sun still peeked over the western horizon. A potbellied, red-faced conductor strolled by and yelled, "Fort Stockton, folks. Next stop is Fort Stockton."

As he stood and gathered up all his personal belongings, Longarm glanced out the nearly opaque windows. Little, if anything, he could see had changed since his last visit to the area. The dusty, windblown village presented no outward indication the U.S. Army even had an active presence within a hundred miles in any direction.

He swung down from the day coach's bottom step and started for the baggage car. The saddle and bedroll awaited him in a neat pile on the almost nonexistent outhouselike depot platform. He dropped his saddlebags on top of the aged McClellan, propped the Winchester against the entire stack, and puffed a cheroot to life.

"I have got to quit these things," he mumbled and then sucked in the first lungful of wondrously satisfying cigar smoke. Seconds later, a nebulous, gun-metal blue ring the size of a washtub floated over his head.

The paunchy-gutted conductor from the El Paso run ambled out of Fort Stockton's pissant-sized depot building and stopped near Longarm. He busied himself by rummaging through what appeared to be a leather-bound notepad for several seconds, then folded the book shut, and glanced over at his former passenger.

"Ain't exactly the Garden of Eden is it?" he said.

Longarm bent at the waist and stretched in an effort to work out some of the travel kinks inflicted by two days of sitting in an uncomfortable train seat. Straightened and said, "Nope. Don't think anyone would ever mistake this part of Texas for God's initial experiment with the creation of mankind."

The conductor removed his cap and wiped a sweaty brow with a kerchief that needed to be washed. "No, sir, wouldn't at that," he grumbled. "You know I still sometimes wonder why I came out to the ass end of the world from Ohio. After considerable thought, I have arrived at the unmistakable conclusion that there must be a goodly amount of mental infirmity running in my family. I've heard passengers say as how this part of West Texas ain't exactly hell, but more'n a few have claimed as how if you ride out to the edge of town, you can actually see the fiery pit 'bout five miles southwest of here."

Longarm offered up a weary smile of approval for the man's feeble attempt at humor. The locomotive's engineer announced departure time had arrived by sending up several short blasts from his ear-piercing whistle. Like an enormous, awakening, South American jungle snake the train slowly came back to life again.

As the stout conductor waddled away he threw a friendly wave Longarm's direction and said, "Well, gotta go. Do be careful, sir. Sulfurous Texas hell can prove out as a mighty dangerous part of the country for a visit." Over his shoulder he absentmindedly added, "Say hello to Satan for me if you happen to see him while you're here." Then he latched onto the moving coach's hand rail, hopped aboard, and yelled out to absolutely no one, "Next stop Sonora. Sonora folks. Next stop Sonora. All aboard for Sonora."

Longarm grabbed up the McClellan, saddlebags, and rifle. From past experience, he knew exactly where to go and followed a pair of age-hardened wagon ruts that ap-

22

peared to wander aimlessly through a mystifying mish-mash of tents, adobe barracks buildings, and crude shacks constructed of little more than pointed sticks hammered into the rock-hard ground.

The overburdened lawman mentally noted that some of the shacks appeared to be used as military housing. Perhaps for the married men, the lawman thought. He knew there had to have been some method to the madness, but what exactly that entailed still evaded him after having visited the place on a number of prior occasions.

Soldiers, who seemed to be totally without any kind of supervision, aimlessly milled about. Camp followers worked at their laundry tubs, rub boards, and clothes lines, while Mexican children with Gringo features ran begging from man to passing man. After a mile or so, the wagon track passed directly by the front gate of the almost nonexistent fort's well-stocked remount stables.

Upon arrival the now thirsty deputy marshal had little trouble finding a uniformed sergeant. He presented his badge, along with letters of introduction and authority signed by the Colorado First District Court's Marshal Billy Vail.

The perspiring lifer barely glanced at either document before he gave them back and offered his hand. "Sergeant Kenneth Ingle, Marshal Long. What can I do to help you out? Be glad to do anything I can by way of assistance, sir."

"That's good to hear, Sergeant Ingle. All too often folks in your position seem bent on making my life more difficult, if they possibly can."

"You've been here before," Ingle said. "More'n once if memory serves. First time I was just a private. Remember as how the stable master at the time said you and the colonel got into a bit of disagreement over the arrival of a telegram by the dispatch rider from Fort Bliss. Course the colonel retired not too long after your visit that time around as I recall. Sergeant Huffines worked my job back then."

"I remember the colonel," Longarm offered. "Hard-shelled, officious fellow name of Ransom, if my sun-baked recollection serves. And while I might well have met the man, can't bring any Sergeant Huffines to mind."

"Oh, I very much doubt you met Huffines. Pretty late in the evening when you got a mount as I remember it. Think Lieutenant Goetz rousted us out that night, but I'd seen you earlier in the afternoon."

"Where's Sergeant Huffines these days? Has he re-tired, too? Moved on to operating a civilian livery of his own?" Longarm wondered aloud.

Ingle cracked a toothy smile. "Nope. As fate would have it, a horse killed him."

Longarm shook his head. "Sweet Merciful Jesus. Get-ting stomped to death is a damned sorry way to go out."

"Don't get too misty-eyed, Marshal Long. Every sol-dier on the post felt the son of a bitch deserved what he got. Most evil man around any kind of animal I've ever known. Big chestnut stallion finally got all he wanted of a daily dose of brutal abuse."

Long kicked at his saddle with the toe of a dust-covered boot. "Yeah, well, I've seen a number of men who got stomped by a horse. Usually one hellacious, bloody mess all the way around."

"Animal named Cyclone done for Sergeant Huffines. Cornered the man back yonder in one of the stalls and kicked the bejabberous hell out of him. One shot. Got 'im right betwixt the eyes with a single, well-placed, steel-shoed hoof." Ingle touched a spot on his own forehead just above the right eye. "Left an absolutely beautiful imprint. Caved ole Huffines's head in like the shell on a hard-boiled egg. Goodly portion of his feeble brains leaked right out on the stall floor."

"My, oh, my," the lawman barely breathed.

"Don't concern yourself overly much. Take my word on the matter, Marshal. Not a soul here at Fort Stockton who knew old Huffines, and especially none of us who had to work with him, mourned that man's violent and providential passing. Come along now, me and my boys will get you fixed up with the best hay burner in the stable."

"Good to hear it."

"Where exactly are you bound today?" Ingle asked as they moved from stall to stall examining the available animals.

"Place named Panther Mountain."

"Ah. 'Bout sixty miles or so south. Easy ride from here. Even in this heat. Not a bad little town."

"Glad to hear it."

"'Course you won't be findin' no panthers anywhere near the place. And the mountain is near 'bouts five miles farther west. But there's some fine folks livin' over that way. Courted a widder woman from Panther Mountain a few years back. Lady had a first-rate ranch and a nice fat bank account. 'Course they've got their share of skunks, too."

"Courtship didn't work out, I take it."

"Lady wanted a feller with a bit more in the way of earthly substance. She married a Panther Mountain banker named Harvey Beerman, as I recall. Son of a bitch had a head like a cue ball, nose like a Mexican parrot, and a belly the size of a flour barrel. Ugly, fat bastard with rotted teeth and a carbuncle on his nose the size of a guinea egg." Both men chuckled at the bizarre image Sergeant Ingle's description conjured up.

25

Eventually Longarm settled on a handsome bay gelding named Stinky that Ingle described as the best seat in the building. Thirty minutes later he'd loaded the animal down with four canteens of water, plenty of beef jerky, bacon, and a dozen flour tortillas purchased at Blake & Blake's General Mercantile.

And, in less than an hour, he and Stinky had traveled far enough down another wagon-rutted track that the miserable, windblown collection of Fort Stockton tents, shanties, and shacks could no longer be seen—even from the highest of West Texas's most barren hills.

Normally, had his business been more urgent, Longarm would have continued pressing south even after the sun had gone down. But the weariness of a two-day train ride and twenty miles in the saddle finally caught up with him. He hobbled the gelding, made camp in a stand of cottonwood trees near an unnamed creek, ate, and stretched out flat for the first time since leaving Denver.

Chapter 4

An hour or so before noon the next day, the sun, now the color of molten steel, along with the harsh, grassless, tree-poor, rolling landscape, had begun to have their naturally debilitating effect on Longarm and the bay gelding. Between them, man and horse had used two canteens of water and started on a third. Longarm poured more of the liquid lifesaver into his hat and offered a taste to the bay.

"Drink up, Stinky. Should be in Panther Mountain soon enough." He glanced out over an inhospitable, barren countryside that rose and fell like a drunken sailor's worst nightmare of a sand-filled ocean. "Think we've gone something over fifty miles, so far. Can't be much more than five or six miles left to our destination I reckon."

The bay slurped down a final tongue-load and Longarm stuffed the soggy hat back on his sweat-drenched head. He patted the gelding on the neck. "Damn sure ain't nothing out here, is there fella? All we've seen is undulating, sand-covered nothingness, burnt-up stunted plants, almost no trees, and a complete absence of water. Oh, and it's hotter than hell under an iron skillet. Soon as we make town, I'm gonna get you and me both out of this sun. Sweet Jesus, ole hoss, it's damned sure a lot cooler in Colorado."

A bit more than an hour later, Longarm reined the tired animal to a halt atop a gentle rise above the outskirts of Panther Mountain. A discolored marker, near the rutted trail, dangled from a wobbly pole and proudly proclaimed a population of 649.

Wind-blistered, sun-bleached clapboard buildings, some enhanced with once showy false fronts painted in gaudy colors, marched north and south in a single line along either side of a wide dirt thoroughfare. The whole shebang, of perhaps thirty to forty buildings total, rested hard in a bowl-like depression by Panther Creek at least five miles east of its forty-six-hundred-foot tall namesake. Here and there, scattered in the brush and scrub, rough, dog-run houses dotted the landscape with most concentrated between the town proper and the lazy, slow-moving creek.

"Looks like the only green spot for miles," Longarm mumbled to himself, then urged his mount forward.

About halfway down the main thoroughfare, he eventually spotted the city jail's modest sign. It also drooped from a disreputable-looking staff as had the marker that announced the obviously dying town's population. Marshal Buster Byers's iron-barred building squatted next to a Mexican café, only a few steps away from a general store called Harlan's Grocery and Mercantile.

Not many people walked the street or boardwalks as the weary deputy U.S. marshal made his way slowly down the street. "Just too hot out for most folks and their animals, I'd bet," he said and stroked the bay's neck.

Longarm carefully noted the location of each business he passed—a once-bustling wagon yard here, what appeared to be an empty, boarded-up saloon there, along with a bakery near Harlan's Grocery and a liquor store directly across the dusty street.

A rooming house on the east side of the rutted dirt roadway had been built almost on top of what appeared the town's only livery and smith operation. Longarm tried to imagine what the smell must be like for boarders who attempted to sleep at night with the pungent, horsey aromas that must waft in from right next door.

He made for the livery, and stepped down just as a hatcheted-faced man in a shirt, pants, hat, and boots, all faded to a shade similar to the man's tired face, limped out to greet him.

The colorless hostler offered a weak, tired smile and said, "Afternoon, mister. Welcome to Panther Mountain. Name's Walker Newman." His speech was as slow as molasses in a Montana winter. He pronounced Newman as two separate words. "You're looking to leave your animal for a spell, I 'spect."

Longarm handed the man his reins. "You'd be entirely correct, Mr. Newman. Might be visiting in your fair town a day or two. Not much longer, I certainly hope. Would like to get ole Stinky here out of the sun. Don't overdo the water or feed though. He's had a long day."

"Well, I can assure you I'll take good care of 'im whilst you're here in Panther Mountain, mister. Downright reasonable on my prices, too. Best attention money can buy won't cost you but a measly four bits a day."

"That'll do just fine. I'll take the saddlebags, bedroll, and Winchester along with me. Can you recommend a clean place to bed down for the night?"

Newman ran dirty-nailed fingers under his hat and scratched. "I'd stay away from Furlong's Roomin' House, next door here, if'n I was you. Place ain't even fit

29

fer my horses, much less folks of quality. And the smell from over this-a-way does get a bit ripe, 'round this time of the year anyways. Used to have a right nice hotel over yonder." He raised a weary arm and pointed to an empty building several doors down from the jail.

"Looks like it's all boarded up," Longarm observed.

"Yes, sir. Closed two or three years ago. But you know, come to think on it, when the moon's just right, and she needs a bit of spare change, old Mrs. Crump lets out a room, once and again. Good lady's a right fine cook, too. Fries about as tasty a chicken as you'll ever put in your mouth. You can get a mighty good meal down there at the Jones Café too. Best pies in Texas, bar none."

"Where's the Crump place?"

"Oh, just follow along Main Street here. Ain't much of a walk. Course, this ain't much of a town. The Crump place is the last house on the left, just past the church. Nothin' between ole lady Crump's and Woods Hollow 'cept maybe thirty miles of stinging sand and scorpions."

"Thanks for the directions, Mr. Newman, and the sound advice. Do appreciate your help. I'll certainly look into the availability of a room at Mrs. Crump's. Can you tell me, though, what happened to your town? Place appears as though it's on its last leg."

"Well, sir, you wouldn't know by looking, but she's only been here a bit over ten years. See, somebody spread a rumor the railroad was a-gonna put in a narrow-gauge spur from Fort Stockton that would terminate right on this very spot. Folks rushed out here, bought land, built businesses, and waited. Those as stuck around, well, they're still a-waitin'. And as you can well see, ain't no railroad."

From inside the stable, a distressed female voice called out, "Pa? Pa? Where's my bridle—the braided

30

horsehair bridle with the silver conchos? I want to go for a ride. Pa? Where are you?"

A second later Longarm glanced toward the stable's open doorway and spotted a red-haired angel marching in their direction. "Oh, there you are. Sorry didn't realize you were talking business, Pa."

Blue-eyed, firm-breasted, and shaped for serious love-making, the girl had squeezed her voluptuous body into the tightest leather riding skirt Longarm had ever seen. The crotch-split garment molded itself to the girl's well-muscled body like a pair of soaked and shrunk men's denim pants.

The flawlessly smooth, tanned face of a woman who spent most of her free time outdoors served to emphasize an upturned nose, and full, naturally red lips that needed no false coloring from the excess application of rouge.

But the most eye-catching part of all her outward beauty, dress, and flair was the barely-laced, thin, blue, chambray blouse she wore. The garment did little to conceal flint-hard nipples surrounded by aroused areolas the size of ten-dollar gold pieces.

Longarm ran his gaze over the strutting female from head to foot, at least twice. He couldn't help but note that almost everything about the eye-catching girl appeared the exact opposite of her wilted, drab father.

"My God," Longarm muttered under his breath.

"Oh, this here is my daughter, Marley Sue," Newman said. "Sorry, mister, didn't catch your name."

Longarm ripped his hat off and flashed his toothiest, most winning smile. "Long. Name's Custis Long, Miss Marley Sue. Mighty pleased to make your acquaintance. My God, yes, I'm mighty pleased."

"This here little gal of mine, well, she's something of a tomboy, as you can probably already see, Mr. Long.

31

Most folks hereabouts just call her Marley 'cause of her boyish ways."

Longarm bowed ever so slightly at the waist. "Then I see no reason to go against what most folks hereabouts do. It's my distinct honor to make your acquaintance, Miss Marley."

Marley Newman seductively sashayed to her father's side and held out a bronze-tanned hand. For the first time, Longarm noticed her flame-tinted tresses appeared to have been cut in a boyish bob with something like a dull butcher knife, or rusty stock shears.

The attention-grabbing female smiled and tilted her leonine head like a large, inquisitive, and dangerous cat. As her fingers clasped Long's, a lightning bolt of searing heat, longing, and unchecked lust, shot up his arm, down his chest, and lodged in a tingling, fiery, knot somewhere below the buckle of his pistol belt. Surprised by the effect she had and his own quick reaction, he flushed, then shifted the saddlebags hanging over his arm, to cover the heat-hardened rod rapidly forming in the crotch of his skin-tight pants.

"Welcome to Panther Mountain, Mr. Long," the girl purred. Her liquid-blue gaze locked onto Long's. As she eased her hand from his, he felt a secret squeeze. Far as he was concerned, the message Marley Newman stealthily conveyed was unmistakable.

Longarm tapped his hat against a sweat-drenched leg. "Most kind of you, Miss Marley."

She ran long, spidery fingers through her hair, then allowed them to casually caress her neck, before she picked at the open lacing of her blouse. "Are you gonna be in town for a spell, Mr. Long?"

"Well, I just mentioned to your father that I'd planned

on two, maybe three, or perhaps even four days. Possibly a week. Depends on what comes up."

A busy fingertip darted across one nipple. "Here on business, Mr. Long?"

"In a manner of speaking, Miss Newman."

"Panther Mountain doesn't get many visiting businessmen anymore. Town's pretty much dried up lately. Used to bustle, bustle, bustle, but not now. What kind of business are you in, Mr. Long? Cattle, cows, land perhaps?"

"No, ma'am, the law. I'm a deputy U.S. marshal. Came in from Denver to take into custody and transfer a prisoner back to Colorado for a fair trial and suitable hanging."

Marley Newman nodded knowingly, then turned and took her own sweet time as she sashayed back toward the stable's open door. She stopped and leaned against the frame in a most sensual and fetching manner.

"Please do be careful while you're visiting our little town, Marshal Long," she growled. "Wouldn't want anything harmful to happen to you. Sure would be a shame to deny the entire female population of Panther Mountain a look at a man like you before you have to go back to Denver." She glanced at his crotch, then winked. "Perhaps we'll see each more of other, later."

"I'll look forward to that happy moment with great anticipation, Miss Marley," replied Longarm as he stuffed his hat back on and noted the damp pool that had gathered in the crotch of his pants.

Marley Newman batted insanely long eyelashes, rolled off the door frame like a cat in heat, and vanished into the deeper darkness of her father's stable. Longarm snatched up his gear and started to walk away.

"There is one other thing that could be of interest to you, Marshal Long," the hostler said.

"And what might that be, Mr. Newman?"

"Given what you just told us, 'bout bein' a lawman and all, I'd make a point of bein' real careful down around the Red Onion Saloon." The older man held Long's inquisitive stare, then added, "If'n I was you, that is."

"Oh. And why would I want to do that?"

"Three, maybe four, evil sons of bitches set up camp down yonder ways day 'fore yestiddy afternoon. Rumors I'm hearin' has it as how they're somehow related to that skunk our marshal has locked up in his jail. Not sure how. Maybe brothers, or cousins, or somethin'. Then again, maybe they're just a bunch of run-of-the-mill killers come to town."

"I'll keep your advice in mind, Mr. Newman. Many thanks." Longarm turned and stared down the almost empty street till he spotted the sun-blasted facade of the Red Onion Saloon. Located six or eight doors past the jail and on the opposite side of the wide thoroughfare, the saloon, with its beveled glass windows sandwiching a set of skewed batwing doors, revealed nothing amiss.

"So far, thank God, them boys ain't brung their animals and trouble up to this end of the street," Marley Newman's father continued. "Most folks is a-sayin' them fellers is probably gonna kill ole Buster and turn his prisoner out. Town's mighty nervous 'bout now. That's why you might've noticed as how there ain't hardly no one out and about this afternoon." As his voice trailed off he added, "That, and a few other things."

Longarm almost asked Newman what he meant by his last remark, but thought better of it. He draped the heavy saddlebags over his shoulder and cradled the Winchester in the crook of his arm. "Well, guess I'd best get along, Mr. Newman." Then, he grabbed up his bedroll and heeled it for the jail.

Chapter 5

A virtually empty street made the short walk from Newman's Livery to the town marshal's office feel like a far greater distance than it appeared. Longarm's creeping unease grew more pronounced with every step. He suddenly realized that he could hear his own breathing, accompanied by the musical jingle and clink of his own spurs.

Panther Mountain's jail was a sturdy, substantial, freestanding building that, on first glance, appeared to have been constructed of railroad ties. The virtually indestructible-appearing fortress squatted between Alphonso's Mexican Café on the south and Harlan's Grocery and Mercantile on the north. Every available window in the crude lockup sported a set of sturdy iron bars attached to the exterior of the edifice with heavy iron screws. The front door looked as though it might be constructed of foot-thick timbers.

Longarm clinked onto the shallow stretch of boardwalk in front of the jail entrance and into the marginal shade offered by a tiny, sloped, covering porch.

The massive portal to the lockup's interior was decorated with a badly weathered wooden sign that had the word MARSHAL, in carefully lettered script, burned into it. The marker hung a bit below eye level. A stubborn latch proved problematic, and the heavy door refused to yield. He leaned forward and knocked.

From inside, Longarm heard someone shout, "Git the hell away, you son of a bitch. Push on my door again and you'll ride a load of heavy-duty buckshot straight to Jesus for judgment. Ain't joshin' with you, goddammit. Go on now. Hit the street a-runnin, and don't be comin' back."

Longarm eased to one side of the plank entry and yelled back, "Marshal Byers, is that you?" No answer. "Marshal Byers, my name is Custis Long. I'm a deputy United States marshal. Your old Texas Ranger comrade Billy Vail sent me down from Denver to retrieve a prisoner at your wired request." Still no answer. "I carry a letter of introduction and other forms of identification, Marshal. If you could just let me inside, or at least open up long enough so I can slip my bona fides to you, I'd be most happy for you to examine them."

Several seconds passed. Nothing of note occurred. Then, heavy, scraping noises emerged from behind the door and, eventually, Longarm heard the sound of at least two large bolts being drawn back. A tiny crack appeared between the facing and the door itself, but the hardly visible gap revealed nothing of the jail's interior.

Someone inside growled, "Just slip yer letter and such right on in here, sonny boy, and I'll sure as hell give 'er a look-see. If'n you ain't tellin' the God's truth, I can gar-un-damn-tee you'll never make it back across Main Street alive."

"Hold your fire now, Marshal Byers. Billy Vail's letter is in my saddlebag. Just hang on while I retrieve it."

Longarm kept his hands where they were easily seen,

slowly squatted, and retrieved a flat, tooled-leather wallet from his saddlebags. He deliberately made quite a show of withdrawing the pertinent paper, and gingerly slipped it through the razor-thin crevice he'd been allowed. The invisible resident snatched the page from his hand, slammed the door closed, and drew at least one of the bolts again.

A few seconds later, the entrance popped open and a man who resembled a starving grizzly bear stepped up to the threshold. He held the letter out and shook it like the paper burned his fingers. Longarm took it.

"You're Long?" the big man barked.

"Deputy United States Marshal Custis Long, your obedient servant, sir. Would I be correct in assuming that I have the honor of addressing Marshal Buster Byers?"

"You would." With a degree of lingering hesitation, Byers offered his pawlike hand and added, "Mighty damned pleased you could make it. Come on inside, sonny. Sent that wire more'n a week ago, as I remember, or maybe it was closer to ten days. I've kinda lost track of time here of late."

"Well, I've been in transit for just over three days, Marshal Byers. Not easy getting here from Denver."

Byers broke the handshake and grabbed up Longarm's bedroll. "Here now, let me help you with your possibles. Let's get off the street. Sure as hell don't wanna give those as might be Hangtown Harry's friends anything to take a potshot at."

In pretty short order, a nervous Buster Byers had helped Longarm move all his personal belongings off the jail's porch, hurriedly ushered his newly arrived guest inside, and bolted the door again.

"How many days you figure on stayin' around, Marshal?"

Longarm let his eyes adjust to the interior darkness. His quick assessment of the town marshal's front office expertly noted a sizable room about fifteen feet deep and twenty feet across. "As many as it takes," he mumbled. "Sure as hell won't head back for a day or so at the very least," he added. Another heavy wooden door that matched the one he'd just stepped through was cut dead center of the back wall. The sturdy entryway, embellished with a foot-square, iron-barred window, obviously led to the jail's cell block.

On one side of the impressive cell house entrance sat a rundown desk and a well-used leather office chair. On the other was an equally disreputable looking bunk bed, a dilapidated ladder-backed chair, and a crude wooden table. The kerosene lamp atop the table offered barely adequate light.

A well-stocked gun rack decorated the wall immediately behind Marshal Byers's desk. Several shotguns, rifles, and a number of pistols—some holstered—burdened the shelves with their deadly weight of powder and iron. Half a dozen keys on a metal ring dangled from a peg on the side nearest the cell block door. Windows on opposite walls of the room, and across the front, were closed and heavily shuttered.

Outside, the midday Texas temperature lingered somewhere near that of a burning boot sitting in Hell's front parlor. Inside the poorly lit, badly ventilated lockup, unmoving, fetid air bordered on stifling.

Longarm dragged his hat off and fanned a dripping face. "Sweet Merciful Jesus, it's hotter than a fresh-forged horseshoe in here. Wonder you haven't gone down from the heat, Marshal. Why've you got the place sealed up so tight?"

Byers let the hammers down on a sawed-off .10-gauge

shotgun, carelessly dropped it on his desk, and flopped into the office chair that appeared to have gone through nearly fifty years of hard use at an extremely busy bank. The cranky seat squeaked, groaned, and complained under the man's massive weight.

"Had 'er opened up like a rollin' taco stand till late yesterday afternoon," he said. "Then a party of Hangtown Harry's friends, or maybe family members, made an unexpected appearance."

"I see. They show nerve enough to come to the jail?"

"Some of the locals said them bold sons of bitches rode right up to the front door yonder. Guess if'n they'd of known I was at home havin' supper at the time, ole Hangtown would already be free as a jaybird and headed back to El Paso."

Longarm jerked a thumb in the general direction of Newman's Livery. "Gent across the street, who owns the livery, told me all about it. Said there might be as many as three, maybe even four of ole Hangtown's *compadres* camped out down at a place named the Red Onion Saloon."

"Yeah," Byers ran the fingers of both hands through ringing wet hair. "That's what I done heard, too. Had folks runnin' in here to tell me all about 'em ever since they arrived. Must be a pretty rotten bunch. Done went and scared hell out of virtually every citizen in the entire town."

"You haven't talked to any of them?"

"Hell, no. Ain't got no reason to confront a bunch of back-shootin' sons of bitches. Most likely they'd just blast the mortal hell out of me, then take Hangtown 'fore I could even bleed out."

Longarm glanced around the sweltering office. Dirty plates, cups, and eating utensils littered almost every flat surface. The rumpled bed very much resembled an extremely large rat's nest. He scratched his chin and almost absently asked, "Don't you have any deputies, Marshal Byers?"

"Had two of 'em, right up 'til yestiddy evenin'. Soon's them yeller-bellied sons of bitches heard 'bout them gunnies down at the Onion, they just naturally threw their badges on my desk and skedaddled."

"Snaked out on you, huh?"

"Yep. That 'ers why I'm all dug in and buttoned down tighter'n an Alabama tick. Hell's bells, cain't watch ever winder in this damned place, all by my lonesome. Was afraid Moon's friends might sneak up and throw a stick of dynamite in on me, or somethin'."

"Sorry to hear about the loss of your deputies," Longarm offered. "But, being as how I'm here now, and can help you with Moon until we can get him out of town, why don't we open all the windows and doors we can? Jesus, Marshal, it's oppressive as Hell's kitchen in July in here." He rubbed his nose and sniffed. "And stinks like an overflowing outhouse."

Byers's chin dropped to his chest. "Haven't been able to get my swamper in here to empty the chamber pots lately. Does reek a bit, I'll admit. But that's mostly because I'm pert sure something crawled up inside ole Hangtown Harry's ass and died. Been havin' to pay two-bits for a Mexican kid to take his pot out back and empty it. Mex sometimes has to use an ax handle to move the stinkin' thing around," he mumbled.

Longarm threw his head back and grimaced. "Sweet Merciful Father, please don't tell me any more."

Byers ignored the request and continued to hack at his excuses. "Ain't nobody been in or out, 'cept the kid for the chamber pots and the feller from next door what brings my food. And all he done, up till now, was set the sacks by the door and run. Hell, Long, wasn't kiddin' in the least when I tole you as how folks 'round here is scared shitless. Right now you could stick a lump of coal up Panther Mountain's collective ass and have a diamond the size of a camel by tomorrow mornin'."

Longarm laughed. And, following some considerable urging, Buster Byers finally gave in, unbolted the heavy inside shutters, and opened all the jail's windows. Within minutes, after removing two chamber pots to an outhouse nearly forty paces behind the jail, and cleaning up most of the collected garbage, the odor had abated considerably. The broiling Texas heat subsided by an entire cooling degree perhaps even two.

Longarm pulled a cheroot and held it between his fingers. "Reckon I could talk with Hangtown Harry now?"

Byers pulled the wooden door open and lifted the key ring from its peg. As he snapped the lock on the inner barred door, he said, "Absolutely. Trust me when I tell you, though, he ain't gonna like you lookin' in on him. Man's the biggest candy ass, complainer, bitch and moan artist, I've ever had locked up in my jail during the entire five years I've been marshal."

The cell block door swung open, and the two lawmen stepped inside. Of the cells, two located on either side of a broad open piece of floor space, three were empty. Hangtown Harry Moon resided in the farthest of the six-by-eight-foot Spartan compartments on the left. The shirtless brigand lay sprawled out in his drawers on a filthy bunk like a fat-bellied, sweaty, unshaven, beached carp.

Longarm stopped a bit more than arm's length from the cell door and said, "My, oh, my, how the once mighty have fallen."

Moon's head lolled toward the voice. "Damn me to an eternal hell if it ain't the Long Arm of the fuckin' law.

41

Shoulda knowed one of you federal boys would show up, sooner or later. Guess you done come all the way to the world's asshole to take me back to Denver for that Phoenix bank job, I 'spect."

"Well, Harry, you and your idiot brother did kill two tellers and the bank manager in the process. Murder, times three, in the process of a robbery that netted you less than a hundred dollars. Guess you might have forgotten such tiny-assed little details."

Hangtown Harry's rheumy eyes rolled up behind half-closed lids. He swung hairless, colorless legs off the bunk, and sat up. "Stupid sons of bitches claimed they couldn't open the damned vault. Time-locked, or some other such nonsense, they said. Didn't get nothin' 'cept the stuff that was left in the cash drawers. Barely pocket change for a man like me."

"Then six months later, you walked into Judge Isaac Mumford's court and shot the man deader 'n Abe Lincoln, after he threw your equally worthless murdering cousin in jail for the rest of his short, sorry, unnatural life, till they hanged him, of course."

"Yeah, done that 'un, too. But, hell, Longarm, nobody in my line of work even bothers to count lawdogs, judges or Messicans. Far as I'm concerned, bastards like you folks ain't nothin' more'n triflin' irritants along life's difficult path—kinda like chiggers or them galling little pussy blisters caused by usin' poison ivy to wipe with."

"Mighty big of you to openly admit your guilt in both bloody matters, especially Judge Mumford's death, Moon. Sounded a lot like a confession to me."

"Well, Mr. Long Arm of the fuckin' law, don't matter a damn what I do, or don't, admit to an irksome little dung-rollin' pismire like you. 'Cause you very simply

42

ain't gonna live long enough to see any benefit from whatever I might tell you now, any damned how."

Longarm almost chewed the cheroot in half. "And just exactly how do you figure that, Harry?"

Moon rubbed, then scratched the hell out of a sweat-drenched, furry belly, and smiled. "Hell, I'm a lot of things, you badge-totin' bastard. Deef ain't one of 'em. Men with my well-bein' at heart arrived in town yestiddy." His voice notched up an octave or more. "Done heard as much from Marshal Buster Be-Goddammned Byers."

"That a fact?"

"Yes, indeed, that's a natural fact. What you boys 've got here is one helluva problem, lawdog. Right good chance you, and this burg's big-assed dunce of a marshal, won't live more'n another day, two at the very most. Soon as you're both graveyard dead and planted, I'll be on my way back to Mexico. Señoritas, *cerveza*, and salsa. Helluva good life down that way."

Longarm shot the smelly killer a cold-eyed look, then flashed a wicked grin. "Well, we'll just see about that, now won't we, Moon. Don't be gettin' your mouth all set for real Mexican tequila and tacos just yet," he said, then turned on his heel and stomped back into the office.

He slammed the cell block door and keyed the heavy lock. "How'd you catch the wretched piece of pond scum, Buster?" he asked and slipped the metal ring back on its wooden peg.

Byers leaned back in his wobbly chair. "On top of all the other problems we've done went and got around here, there's only two functionin' combination saloon-dancehall-gamblin' establishments left."

"I spotted a number of such boarded up buildings along the street on the way over today."

"Yeah. Well, competition for business in a dyin' economy has done got right intense of late. Been several back and forth shootin's, killin's, and such, 'tween 'em. Several months ago, the owner of the Wagon Wheel hired a gunny name of Braxton Pike. Well, that ripped the rag right off the bush. Proprietor of the Red Onion went and brought ole Hangtown in to even things out a bit. Guess they both figured as how no one this far out of the mainstream would recognize the murderous skunk."

"But, naturally, you did."

"Knew all about ole Moon's infamous reputation from my Rangerin' days. Caught the vile snake in the alley comin' out of the Onion's back door, one night a week or so ago. Hell, he was drunker'n Cooter Brown."

"Give you much trouble?"

"Not really. Hell, I snuck up from behind, and whacked him a time or two with an ax handle."

"Well, that should have done the job."

"Tell the truth, Marshal Long, the man's got a skull like an anvil. And bein' as how I had a wanted dodger right here on my desk that offered two thousand dollars cash money for his capture, I knew exactly who to wire. Had ole Hangtown locked up back there ever since."

"You can't have believed that no one would come and try to help him."

"Oh, I kinda figured someone *might* show up. But I also knew how bad Billy Vail, and you federal boys, wanted him for killin' that judge. Thought sure you'd get here quicker than his friends or family though."

"Well, it is a ways from Denver down to the backside of hell."

"Understand completely. But I'd surely appreciate it if you could wire Billy soon as you get back to Fort Stockton and certify that I did, for damned sure, capture the real, honest-and-for-damned certain Hangtown Harry

Moon and have him in my custody. Would like my money wired back, right quick-like. Plan to spend at least some before his stupid brothers, or evil *compadres*, kill me deader'n a rotten fence post."

A hard-edged testiness crept into Longarm's voice when he shot back, "Don't worry, Marshal Byers, you'll get your money. I'll personally see to it."

"Always worry when it comes to money, Long. Especially when it amounts to as tidy a sum as two thousand dollars."

Longarm pulled his hat off, fanned his face again, and moved toward the door. "Little bit of a breeze we're getting now helps with the heat, but not much. Seeing as how I'm here to help out, reckon we could even open the front and back doors as well. Might get something in the way of better exposure to some cross ventilation from the available moving air that way. Sure as hell couldn't hurt any. Nothing much bad happened when you opened the windows now did it?"

The words had barely passed Longarm's lips when a booming voice from the street cut through the muggy air like a bolt of silver-blue, pitchfork lightning during a summer thunderstorm. "Get yore sorry ass out here, Byers. Come on, now. Buck up and take yore medicine."

A whiskey-slurred second voice yelped, "Come on out here and get it. It's yer time to eat the weasel, fur, teeth, toe nails, and all."

Then the boomer added, "Shit. We aim to kill the hell out of yew, big boy. Then we're gonna set Hangtown Harry Moon loose."

A third voice, that sounded like it came from the bottom of a grave, growled, "And when we're done with you, gonna burn this festerin' pile of cow shit you call a town to the goddamned ground."

Chapter 6

Longarm's hand darted to the oiled walnut grip of his Colt Frontier model double-action pistol. He eased to a sheltered spot near the door and peeked out one of the office's now-open front windows. His gaze fell immediately on a villainous cur he recognized.

Over his shoulder he barely breathed, "The one in the middle is none other than One-Eyed Charlie Tatum. Man's bad news if there ever was any."

"Know 'im?"

"We're not exactly on speaking terms. But there's no way to miss that black leather patch covering one whole side of the brigand's butt-ugly, bear-clawed face. Don't recognize either one of the other two. The hostler, Newman, said he thought some of Moon's family might be in town, but I don't see any of them."

Marshal Byers slid quietly to Longarm's side. "Moon does have a number of brothers, as you probably well know. All of 'em are equally villainous. And if they ain't here in town this very minute, you can rest assured they will be."

"You recognize either of the other two men out there right now, Buster?"

"Hook-nosed, pale feller on the left, that look's like he died last week, is a Texas killer named Whitey Kilgore."

"He's a sickly-looking devil all right."

"Git close enough, Marshal Long, and you'll see the ugly sucker has pink eyes. Most folks believe he's an albino."

"Killer, you say, Buster?"

"Yes, sir. Be willing to bet my next month's pitiful-assed Panther Mountain marshal's pay, ole Whitey's murdered at least a dozen people. Just in the past year. Can't see the third feller's face under that palm-leaf sombrero. He's carryin' a mighty fancy bone-gripped pistol behind his sash. Shit, that 'un could be anybody."

One-Eyed Charlie Tatum shook a bottle of whiskey at the jailhouse window and yelled, "Yew ain't foolin' nobody, Byers. Me and the boys see yew creepin' 'round in there. Git yer big, broad ass out here in the street, right by God now. Cain't run and hide no longer. Gotta step up and deal with the consequences of yer own uncommon fuckin' stupidity."

Byers barely heard Long when, from between teeth clamped down hard on a nickel cheroot, he growled, "I've heard enough of this. Grab your shotgun, Buster. Pull one of those in the rack down and load it for me."

In a matter of seconds, both lawmen had armed themselves with sawed-off, double-barreled, .10-gauge, man-killing Greeners, and stood expectantly behind the jailhouse door.

"Here's how we'll handle this dance," Longarm said. "You go left, I'll go right. When we get outside, we'll move up to the edge of the boardwalk as close to those boys as we can. Closer we get to them, the less likely they'll be to do anything foolish. Once we're settled and ready, let me do the talking."

Byers's short, thick fingers nervously gripped and regripped his weapon. "Sure. You go right on ahead. Talk all you want. Sounds good enough to me." His eyes darted around the room like a man about to pass out.

"Calm down, Buster. Let's be smart about this thing. Don't do any shooting, unless absolutely necessary. If anything wayward occurs that threatens both of us, blast the man nearest you. I'll get the other two. Otherwise, let me take care of any action from individual big behavers. Are we clear? Do you understand?"

Longarm stared into the Panther Mountain marshal's wobbly eyes. Didn't particularly like the obvious cloud of fear and confusion he saw brewing there. "Are you still with me, Buster? Did you grasp what I just said?"

For several more seconds, Byers looked bewildered and something more than a bit unnerved. Finally, he nodded and said, "Hell, yeah, I heard you. Understood everything you said."

"Fine. Just checking. You're gonna have to be sharp for me now."

Byers stared at his hands as though he couldn't see them. He still gave the impression of not having heard any of Longarm's admonitions, and said, "Just be aware that I've not taken part in anythin' like a real gunfight in more'n ten years."

"Well, damnation, Buster. You might have thought about that before you whacked Hangtown Harry across the noggin' with an axe handle. But, that's okay. Most likely this won't develop into an exchange of gunfire anyway. Have to be mighty stupid to draw on a man facing you with a shotgun."

"All that kind of behavior stopped when my Ranger days come to an end, you know. Hell's bells, a *town* marshal, out here on the raw edge of forever, don't do much more'n keep the streets clean of horse shit, lock up the town drunks, run truants back to school, shoot stray dogs, make sure the pigs don't create a waller in the middle of Main Street, and such like."

"I understand, but you need to get a grip on your emotions before we step outside."

Byers couldn't let his train of thought loose. "Bein' marshal of a town like Panther Mountain's a nice, easy, safe job. That's why I like it, you know. Never thought takin' ole Hangtown down would come to somethin' like this, Long. Honest to God, I didn't. Thought sure he'd be gone by now anyway. At 'ere reward musta screwed with my normally sound judgment, in matters like this 'un."

Longarm again locked eyes with the obviously agitated lawman. "Do like I told you, Buster, and it'll all work out fine as frog hair. You know, as well as I do, that being a bit anxious in a situation like this is normal. Just don't freeze up on me once we get onto the boardwalk. Now, open the door and follow me outside."

"I've got a wife and kids, you know. Even got a couple of grandkids." Byers moaned. "Shit. Like I said, only took ole Hangtown down 'cause of the reward money. Now look at this mess. Got killers right here on the doorstep of my jail."

"Cock your weapon and follow my lead. Don't worry yourself overmuch. These men can't be stupid enough, or drunk enough, to go up against this kind of firepower. Shotguns at the distance we'll be working from aren't to be argued with. Even ole Charlie isn't stupid enough to draw when confronted with four loads of heavy-gauge buckshot." With that, Longarm took charge, pulled the door open, stepped onto the boardwalk, and moved up to its edge. Marshal Byers trailed behind and fidgeted with his weapon.

One-Eyed Charlie Tatum's only workable orb popped open to about the size of the bottom of a pewter beer mug. He squinted hard, rubbed his one good eye with the back of a greasy hand and said, "Just who'n the hell 'er yew, yew shotgun-carryin' son of a bitch?"

"I'm surprised, and hurt, you don't recognize me, Charlie. Such unthinking memory loss cuts me right to the quick. Try using your head for a second, you ugly gob of spit. Think. Custis Long, deputy United States marshal from Denver. Remember?"

Whitey Kilgore sucked down a horse-killing slug from his bottle, smeared whiskey-moistened lips on the back of a filth-encrusted sleeve, then snapped, "Hell, I doan care a goddamn who in the sulfurous hell yuh are, yuh long-legged son of a bitch. Yuh ain't got no dog in this 'ere hunt, mister, no cock in this fight, no business messin' in our business."

Longarm let the open barrel of the big blaster roam back and forth, from one man to the next. "You're dead wrong on that count, Whitey. I'm here on instructions from United States Marshal Billy Vail to take Hangtown Harry Moon back to Denver for trial and suitable hanging. Marshal Byers has got absolutely no say in the matter."

Whitey had the floor and seemed to thrive on the attention. "Step aside and let us hammer this little pissant disagreement out with ole Buster yonder, *Deputy* Marshal Long. He's the one what done went and locked our friend Hangtown Harry up."

"What's your stake in this Whitey?" Longarm asked.

"Moon's brothers sent us on ahead to see if we could work this out 'fore they ride on in from back El Paso way.

Had other business, yuh see. Trust me when I say, yer badge-totin' boys would a lot rather deal with me, Willy, and Charlie than that bunch of mad-dog vicious sons of bitches."

The man in the palm-leaf sombrero finally tilted his head back. Stunned by what he saw, Longarm took a half step back, and brought his heavy weapon to bear directly on the newly exposed threat.

As the brim of the hat came up, a massive nose, broken numerous times, in countless fights, slowly appeared. The badly flattened snout was flanked on either side by one blue eye and one brown eye. The odd pair of eyeballs were so severely crossed Longarm had trouble telling exactly what the man was looking at, if anything.

"Well, well, well, if it isn't Willy Coffin, I'll eat my saddle. Won't even have to boil it," Longarm said. "You've roamed a bit far from your old stomping grounds there, haven't you, Willy? I've always heard you did most of your back-shooting over in New Mexico Territory."

Coffin pulled at the buckle of his gun belt, adjusted the pistol strapped high on his hip ever so slightly. Ashes dropped onto the killer's shirt front from the half-burned panatela that dangled from his curled lips. "I go, by God, wherever in the hell I please, Long. Don't give a damn what dung eaters like you think either."

"Be that as it may, Willy, you're sure as hell in the wrong place, at the wrong time today."

"You know, Charlie," Coffin snarled, "it's days like this 'un what make me think there just might well be an actual God up there in them cloudless Texas heavens."

"And how's that, Willy?" One-Eyed Charlie sneered. "Tell us all why yew mighta done gone and become a true believer."

"Well, any time I get delivered up of an opportunity to

kill a man I've wanted to rub out for years, it just makes me thankful all to hell, you know. Sweet Jesus, I just might have to visit a church later on today and offer up a prayer of righteous thanks for such heavenly intervention. Hell, I might even have to put somethin' in the plate to show my sincerity."

All of a sudden, Longarm could hear Buster Byers's labored, ragged breathing. Near as he could tell, something in the poor man's fevered brain bordered right on the verge of snapping.

"No need for gunplay, boys," Longarm offered. "I didn't come here after any of you. Got no wants, warrants, or papers of any kind. So, why don't all you gents just mosey on off, get on your horses, ride the hell out of town, and don't bother to come back."

Willy Coffin's hand darted for the Remington pistol hanging in the single-loop, Mexican holster on his thick, double-row cartridge belt. The outlaw's fingers had barely stroked the cut-bone grips when Longarm touched off a single, thunderous, ear-splitting barrel of .10-gauge buckshot. A tight group of well-aimed lead balls smacked the gunman in the chest. The fistlike lick sent him staggering two steps backward in a cloud of spent black powder that rolled from the boardwalk like a high plains thunderhead spitting lightning.

Coffin's hurried, drunken, cross-eyed grab for his pistol resulted in a misplaced shot that blew a hole in the top of his own foot. The combined report from both weapons, fired in such close sequence and proximity, ricocheted off the glass windows of every storefront in town, sped down Main Street, and headed for Mexico.

A fist-sized wad of tissue, bone, blood, and rendered cloth exited the surprised brigand's back, just below his left shoulder blade. Vaporized clouds of sticky gore still hung in the air when Coffin's body hit the ground and flopped around the dusty street in a spasm of stunned, eye-popping death. Mere seconds later, the man ceased moving as his life spewed into the waiting earth.

Charlie Tatum, his one good eye about to pop out of his head, flung the whiskey bottle aside, threw up both hands and screeched, "Christ Almighty, don't shoot. Don't shoot any more, Marshal. Please, God, I'm gettin' on my knees. Gettin' down on my knees. Ain't touchin' my weapon."

Spiritual fervor seemed the order of the moment. Whitey Kilgore got religion for the first time in his entire wretched life. "Sweet merciful, Jesus," he cried as his shaky hands shot into the air. "Ain't touchin' my pistol, Marshal. Please God don't shoot that big popper off no more. Christ on a crutch, yuh done gone an' damn near blew ole Willy in half. Shit, fuckin' fire."

Longarm held the shotgun in one hand, covered the cowering gunmen, and motioned Marshal Byers forward. "Go get their pistols, knives, and other instruments of death-dealing and destruction, Buster. Make damned sure you give each of them a careful going-over. They've most likely got some kind of hidden weapons on them. For Christ's sake, be thorough. Don't want one of them coming up with something you missed and killing you or me."

Chapter 7

Within a matter of seconds after Willy Coffin hit the dirt, Panther Mountain's previously empty main thoroughfare filled with a buzzing mob of people who poured from the entranceway of every building that wasn't closed or boarded up. Shopkeepers, bartenders, ranch hands, housewives, and painted bawdy women milled around like thirsty cattle looking for water.

Most of the gawkers crossed their arms over their chests, and stared open-mouthed at Willy Coffin's shattered corpse as it oozed blood, and other bodily fluids, into the dusty, wind-blown street. Some pointed and nervously laughed at the piss spot on the front of his pants. Others hid their mouths behind cupped hands, shook their heads as though in a state of stunned and shocked disbelief.

The crowd eventually got so dense, one drunken cowboy staggered up to the outer ring of gapers and loudly complained, "Some of y'all should step aside, goddammit. Them as have seen the dead man should make a place for newcomers to view the bloody tragedy. Those of us in the back has just as many rights as the rest of you sons of bitches, you know."

Someone who had a prime spot in front yelped, "Aw, shut the hell up. Go back to your nose paint, you brush-poppin' bastard."

Undeterred, the inebriated waddie calmly replied, "We've got just as much right to look at the corpse of the poor stupid son of a bitch as any of you other'ns who think you're so damned superior. Come on, now. Let folks what ain't seen the stiff have a look."

When the crowd finally parted and the loud-mouthed leather pounder got his much desired peek at the shattered heap that had been Willy Coffin, he blanched and said, "Jesus H. Christ, 'at 'eres one helluva big hole in his chest, ain't she? And, God Almighty damn, look at all the gore. Sure 'nuff's a lot of blood, piss, and other stuff in a man with a melon-sized cavity in him, ain't they?"

Marshal Byers dumped six pistols, of various types and calibers, four knives, a set of brass knuckles, and a lead-filled leather sap on the boardwalk at Longarm's feet. "What 'cha want me to do with these bastards now?" he said.

"You've got three empty cages available back there in your cell block, Marshal Byers. Lock their sorry asses up, but make sure you put them in separate cells."

"Lock 'em up? What for? They ain't really done nothing 'cept got drunk and mouthed off some. Neither one of 'em pulled a pistol. We ain't got no judge in town, so the best I can do is maybe fine 'em for public intoxication and turn 'em loose once they're sober. Lest maybe we can ferret out some wanted posters on 'em."

"That's good enough for right now, Buster. If we have to let them go later on, so be it. But for right now, and until they're sober, we'll keep these two churnheads under lock and key. Just two more things we won't have to worry ourselves about for a spell."

As Byers marched his newly-acquired prisoners into the jail, and the town's gaping onlookers continued their unfettered inspection of the recently departed Willy Coffin, Marley Newman strolled up. She glanced at the corpse, gritted her teeth, and shook her head. Then turned and smiled at Longarm like he was the only man on earth.

"Well, well, well, Marshal Long," she said, "you sure as shootin' didn't waste any time getting the entire town's undivided attention, did you?"

Longarm breeched the shotgun, extracted both rounds of brass, snapped it shut again, and propped the weapon against a wooden porch pillar. "Swear to Jesus, I tried my level best to avoid any kind of a fight, Miss Marley. Don't care to shoot a man unless it's just unavoidable. Even went so far as to offer Willy Coffin what I felt was an easy way out. But dodging a scrap is right hard to do when men, like ole Willy, come looking hell-bent for a killing. As far as I'm concerned, the dim-witted skunk took his own life when he made an ill-conceived grab for his weapon. Could have walked away and still be alive. Just can't account for raw, unrestricted stupidity."

"Well, I'll put it another way then, Marshal. Sure got my attention," she purred and slyly brushed one breast against his arm.

As Longarm watched the girl strut away, a solemn-faced man in a badly used black suit and worn-out stovepipe hat glided into his line of sight like a cloud of vapor blown across water on a warm spring morning. The ghostly stranger blocked his view of Marley Newman's swaying, come-hither ass.

In an otherworldly, almost disembodied voice, the

gaunt-faced specter removed his tall hat, presented Long-arm with a printed calling card, and said, "My name is Joshua Smoot, sir. I am the owner-operator of Smoot's Furniture, Undertaking, Funeral Parlor, Veterinary, Barber Shop, and Bath House."

Longarm glanced at the card. "Looks like you arrived on the scene at just the right time, Mr. Smoot."

Smoot ran a long-fingered hand over the two or three hairs left on his oily, liver-spotted skull. "I must confess to having witnessed the recent events that transpired here from my window yonder, sir. Set me to wondering if, perhaps, you might be in need of my professional assistance."

Longarm tried but couldn't avoid the humor of such an ill-phrased question. "Don't think I'm personally ready to get planted just yet, Mr. Smoot. But the feller stretched out over there, in the street, the former Mr. Willy Coffin, could definitely benefit from your services."

Joshua Smoot placed the stovepipe hat back on his head, laced boney fingers together, and, in a pose of deep thought, held his hands against a skeletal chest. "Smoot's Funeral Parlor would be most happy to oblige in any way we can, sir. However, during these times of trauma and anxiety, we're always forced to discuss the somewhat repellent pecuniary details involved in any professional handling of the recently departed's mortal remains."

Longarm used one finger to push his hat onto the back of his head. "Alright, let's get to the final ledger entry, Mr. Smoot. What's the freight for sending a skunk like ole Willy off to a sure-fire meeting with Satan?"

Smoot dipped into the pocket of his faded-black waistcoat, whipped out a dog-eared, leather-bound notebook, thoughtfully thumbed from page to page for several seconds, and said, "For our standard, no-frills buryin', Smoot's Undertaking and Funeral Parlor charges ten dollars, plus five dollars for a cloth-lined, hand-hewn, wooden coffin constructed by a master Mexican furniture maker. Grand total of all related expenses in planting the dead man comes to fifteen dollars."

Longarm nodded his approval. "Tally sounds reasonable to me."

"As I am also minister at the local church, that humble price includes a graveside religious service. I personally conduct the sacraments myself. I'm accompanied by three professional mourners. They attend the ceremony to make certain even the most despicable of the recently deceased get off to their just reward with proper recognition of their earthly departure—whatever that might entail. It's a right fine rendition of the proper ritual, even if I do say so myself."

"Look now, as far as I'm concerned, you can remove whatever you find on the body—guns, money, boots, clothing, and such. Pretty sure he's got a horse and saddle somewhere—and you can put the monies derived from the disposal of all those earthly goods toward payment of any funerary fees. Hell, I'd bet that Remington pistol ole Willy tried to use on me should be worth at least three times your normal charge for putting a man in the ground."

Smoot thought the proposition over for a second, then nodded. "Such an arrangement would seem most equitable and agreeable, sir. I'll have Mr. Coffin's mortal remains in the ground as quickly as possible—if everything goes well, by tomorrow morning at the very latest."

"That sounds just fine as frog hair as well."

"Otherwise, any substantive delay in this stifling heat and he'll get ripe real quick. The smell can be a bit off-putting, as you well know, I'm sure."

Longarm decided the conversation had gone on long

enough. He tipped his hat and said, "My sentiments exactly, sir. You go right ahead and put ole Willy in the ground fast as you can. If for no other reason, just to make certain the vile son of a bitch is good and dead."

With a flourish, Smoot grandly slipped the tattered notebook back into his waistcoat pocket. "You look like a man who could use a good shave and hot bath, yourself, Marshal. Come by Smoot's Bath House anytime. We're open until ten o'clock every evening. Heat water drawn directly from Panther Creek. Good soak in our mountain water is fully guaranteed to restore the morale and raise the spirits."

The gaunt undertaker turned like an infantry drill sergeant, motioned to a boy across the street, and snapped his knotted, bony fingers. The raggedly-dressed, dirty-faced urchin dragged a two-wheeled cart to Willy Coffin's side, dropped the tongue, and appeared to stand at attention while he awaited further instructions.

Smoot glanced at Longarm once more, and as if to drive the bath-house sales point home said, "Stop by at your convenience, sir. Shave, haircut, and bath, only six bits. There is, of course, a nominal fee for imported after-shave tonics, colognes, and other *additions* to our standard service."

Smoot performed a barely visible bow, then hurried to the corpse. Long watched as the rail-thin, ghostly apparition single-handedly got the carcass loaded on the wagon, and disappeared with it so fast Long wondered if he'd actually seen the whole performance transpire. As soon as the dead man vanished, in a cloud of fine dust and the squeak of metal wheels, so did most of the rowdy crowd.

Longarm continued to stand watch from the jail's rickety porch. Shotgun at the ready, he kept his station until everyone who wanted a viewing of the death scene had strolled past the bloody spot in the dirt, pointed at it, pointed at him, discussed the horror of the shooting, and moved on to whatever else their lives required. For most of that time he wondered what Smoot meant by other *additions* to his standard barbering service. It proved an intriguing question to mull over on a hot afternoon.

Within a matter of minutes the only sounds that could be heard on Panther Mountain's main thoroughfare were the rinky-tink piano music from both saloons, and the raucous laughter of those celebrating the fact that they were lucky enough to still reside amongst the living.

Chapter 8

Buster Byers keyed the lock on the barred gate to the cell block and snapped it shut. He slammed the wooden outer door and threw the iron bolt into its socket, then turned to watch as Longarm settled the Greener back into its slotted place in the rough jail's overflowing gun rack.

"Well now, Marshal Long, I ain't done no stand up gun work in years. Cain't say as I've missed the experience the least bit. Damned if I ain't still shakin'. Never cared for the prospect of gettin' shot at, even back in my younger days as a Ranger down in Del Rio and Eagle Pass."

Longarm moved around Byers's desk and flopped down on the ladder-backed guest chair's ragged seat. "There's just nothing can quite match facing ole bony-fingered death to get a man in touch with the way he really feels about life, mortality, and the Great Beyond—is there, Buster?"

Byers dropped the jingling ring of keys onto its peg and lowered his enormous bulk into the leather-covered chair behind his desk. He pulled a faded blue bandanna and wiped out the inside of his hat. "Yeah, well, to tell the God's truth, feel like I already done enough gun fightin' some years ago. Would prefer not to have to go through another'n like what we just done today anytime soon."

Longarm pulled a cheroot and lit it. "If I remember correctly," he said, then sucked in a lung of the calming smoke and blew it at the ceiling, "you're the one that got bold enough to whack Hangtown Harry with an ax handle, snatch his unconscious ass up, and throw him in your jail. And like I said before, you should've figured there'd be trouble coming."

Byers closed his eyes and appeared beset by a sharp, severe pain somewhere behind his eyes. He rubbed his forehead and said, "Yeah, well, I guess maybe the thought of all that reward money might have blinded me to the absolute reality of the bloody situation."

Longarm thumped ashes on the floor. "What's done is done, Buster. The *situation* is what it is, and we're just gonna have to deal with it."

"I suppose." Byers wagged his head back and forth like a confused steer. "Not to change the subject on you, but have you found a place to stay for the night?"

"Not yet. Walker Newman warned me away from the hotel. But he did mention a lady named Crump that might have a room available. Said the good woman cooked a mighty tasty chicken."

"No need to spend money on a room. You can bed down right here at the jail. Take that'n over yonder."

Long eyeballed the lumpy cot, scratched his chin and said, "Don't know about that, Buster. I'm looking for a good night's rest. Bet sleeping in that thing is like rolling around in a rock-filled cocklebur patch."

"No, truly. You can trust me on this, Marshal Long. I know it looks pretty rough, but believe me, it sleeps just great. And it's right easy to get a fine meal if you bunk here. The Mexican joint next door's got damned good food. Or, if you prefer, there's the Jones Café just a short walk down the street. Lady who runs the Jones makes the damnedest pies you done ever tasted. Puts a tasty crust on a piece of beefsteak, too. Saloons have free lunches available to patrons who buy a drink."

Longarm raised an eyebrow. "Guess I can take it you won't be sleeping here tonight."

"Nope. Not a chance. Long as you're gonna be here for a day or so, I'm goin' home, fast as I can hoof it."

"Where's home?"

"Got a nice little spread 'bout five miles south of town. I ain't laid eyes on my kids for three days. Wanta sleep with my ole lady tonight. Figured as long as you're in town, you could have the office all to yerself. Know it ain't much, but it's a site better'n nothin', and a whole lot better'n that stinkin' hotel."

Longarm glanced around the room. He mentally calculated it would take another hour or more to sweep out, finish cleaning up, and make the place passably livable. "What about the prisoners, Buster?" He glanced around the office and noted the presence of a broom standing in the corner behind Marshal Byers's desk.

"What about 'em?"

"Well, I suppose you do feed your inmates, don't you?"

"Aw, hell, don't be worrin' yourself none about that. Armondo Diez, from next door, brings tortillas refried beans, and such, twice a day." Byers waved at the jail-house door as though Diez stood right outside at that very moment.

"He must be due soon then."

"Yep. Sun's gonna go down in another hour or so. He should be here right quick." He waved at the door again.

"You obviously trust the man."

"Oh, hell, yes. You'll like Armondo, Marshal Long. Nice feller for a Mex. And his food's mighty good. Best part is he always brings plenty. I usually take my meals from whatever he's got left, if I'm here. But you do as you please. Set yourself up however you want. Rearrange the office, any way you care to, if you like. Don't make no never mind to me, one way or t'other."

"Anything else?" Longarm asked.

Byers reached for the door latch, hesitated, ran a hand under his hat and scratched his head, then said, "Oh, yeah. Just so you'll know, they's a Mexican kid with a big ole dog sleeps under the front porch sometimes. Ain't got no family as I know of. Name's Jesus Sanchez. He's my swamper. Empties the chamber pots in the cells, sweeps out some, picks up trash and generally takes care of the place. I let Armondo feed him for his labors. Anything you want, just check with Jesus. You need me, send Jesus. I'll get back here quick as I can."

"Sounds good."

"Do be careful 'round his dog though. Big son of a bitch bites, and once he latches on he's worse'n a Mississippi River snappin' turtle. Harder'n hell to get him loose."

"That the whole of it? Nothing else I need to know?" Longarm rubbed his chin to cover a grin.

"Oh, there is one other thing. If you go out, use this here big ole padlock on the front door. Might not keep anyone that's real determined outside, but it should slow 'em down a bit. Key's right up here on this nail."

"Are you sure that's necessary? We've already got those boys behind two locked doors as it is."

For several seconds Byers got the look of a puzzled grizzly before saying, "You're probably right. I'uz just thinkin' out loud. Tryin' to figure the worst what could very well happen."

"Ever had anyone break into your jail in an effort to take a prisoner out?"

"As a pure matter-of-fact, no. But I ain't never had anyone like Hangtown Harry, Whitey Kilgore, or One-Eyed Charlie Tatum locked in my jail before, neither." With that, Panther Mountain's marshal offered a half-hearted wave and heeled it for the street.

About an hour after Byers left, Longarm finally got the office completely swept out, picked up, and rearranged to suit his sensibilities, comfort, and most immediate personal needs. He ripped the filthy sheets off the cot, and carried the mattress outside for a serious whacking with the broom, then threw his own bedding down over the well-used mattress. Once whacked and fluffed, he had a clean, comfortable bed that beat the hell out of a room in Panther Mountain's only hotel, sleeping on the floor, or camping on the ground with every scorpion in south Texas.

A smiling Armondo Diez showed up right on time, and knew exactly what to do about feeding the prisoners. He nodded, grinned, bowed, motioned at the keys, and let himself into the cell block.

Longarm stood guard at the door and watched as the Mexican cook served each man from an oblong metal pan filled with tortillas, frijoles, grilled meat, and a variety of vegetables and peppers.

One-Eyed Charlie Tatum was up in a shot, hung on the

bars, and yelped, "*Mas, mas, muy mas,* you Messican bandit. I'm hungry, goddammit. *Mas, amigo.*"

Whitey Kilgore laid on his cot like a man who'd been in Buster Byers's jail for years. He glanced at the tin plate shoved under his cell door, threw Longarm a sickly look, but didn't appear anywhere close to being interested in eating.

Longarm couldn't help but smile when he heard Tatum say, "Hell, you don't want them frijoles, Whitey? You just slide 'em on over here. My poor stomach's emptier'n a El Paso banker's heart."

Kilgore sat up long enough to say, "Yer stomach is always empty, Charlie. Yuh eat more and stay harder to fill up than any man I've ever been around. Sometimes think as how maybe yer related to a cow and have two stomachs or, at the very least, yer plagued with a tapeworm the size of a water trough."

Hangtown Harry sounded like a man in the throes of some horrible disease. He rolled his eyes at Armondo and moaned, "Oh, bloody hell. You're back again? I ain't had nothin' to eat but them Messican strawberries now for nigh on two weeks."

"*Sí, señor. Es muy bueno,*" said the still-grinning Armondo.

Moon banged his head on the cell door. "Hell, no it ain't *bueno*. Christ, I need some beefsteak smothered in about two pounds of fried onions, taters, squash, maybe some green beans and corn bread."

Armondo slipped the food under Hangtown Harry's cell door. Moon snatched the tin plate off the floor and stared at the contents like he might retch. "Much as I hate 'em, guess this is all we're gonna git, boys. Best go ahead on and eat, Whitey. These thunder-makin' little bastards is better'n nothin', I suppose."

Once he'd escorted Armondo back to the street, Longarm got a change of clothing from his saddlebags, made sure his prisoners were locked down tight, padlocked the front door, and headed for Smoot's bath and barber shop.

Chapter 9

As Longarm stepped from the jail's rickety porch steps, the formerly bustling street had reverted back to its almost empty status. Small, boisterous, knots of men and a few women had congregated around the entrances of both saloons.

He cut a wary gaze along the storefronts and alleyways of the nearly vacant street, then hoofed it across Panther Mountain's main thoroughfare to Smoot's tonsorial shop. The afternoon's energy-stealing heat had started to let up, just a bit, as a blood-red bubbling sun settled in the west.

A tiny, silver bell above the beveled-glass door jingled when he entered the shop. Joshua Smoot's lanky, scarecrow-like form was draped over the only available chair. The combination undertaker, embalmer, veterinarian, barber, and bathing facility owner sat up, then stood and rubbed sleep-filled eyes. In an unexpected burst of oddly graceful speed, he nimbly stationed himself behind the leather-padded chair and motioned for Longarm to take a seat.

"I've been waiting. Felt sure you'd be along sometime

71

this evening, sir. Have a bath being prepared for you at this very instant. Put your change of clothing on that chair yonder, if you'd like, Marshal. Have a seat, and I'll shave you before you bathe."

In pretty short order, it became apparent that Joshua Smoot practiced barbering as though it were an art form. For about thirty sublime minutes, Longarm knew, beyond any doubt, he had fallen into the hands of a talented expert at the trade.

He blissfully soaked under a series of steaming hot towels, scented with something pleasantly restful that he couldn't quite recognize. When the skin of his weathered countenance had apparently achieved just the right degree of suppleness, the taciturn Mr. Smoot proceeded with the application of a rolling cream massage that seemed to go on for hours. Then Smoot carefully soaped the tired lawman's face and began the razor work.

About midway through the shave, Longarm said, "In your opinion, Mr. Smoot, what's the real secret to a great shave?"

The cadaverous barber smiled. "A sharp razor is the answer, my good sir, along with an exceptionally steady hand." Smoot stopped, wiped foamy soap from the glistening blade onto the towel laid over his shoulder, then slowly, expertly, ran it up and down the leather strop. First one side, then the other. "Keep mine keen enough to take a man's head off with one clean, quick stroke." He gingerly touched the edge with his thumb. "Yes, sir. You just can't beat a sharp razor, Marshal Long."

A few minutes later Longarm stood and gazed at his newly scraped reflection in the mirror behind the chair. He rubbed his cheek and chin with a towel, then slapped witch hazel on his freshly shaved face.

"Do believe that's the closest shearing I've ever had, Mr. Smoot," he said by way of a compliment.

Smoot's corpselike mouth spread into an appreciative grin. He snapped the ivory-handled razor closed and said, "Of course, sir. No question at all, without any doubt, the closest shave you've ever had. My personal guarantee on it. Now, marshal, if you'll fetch your change of clothing and please follow me."

Longarm retrieved his fresh duds and trailed Smoot through a doorway in the back wall of the shop and down a narrow hallway. At the second door off the tight passage, the affable barber stopped and motioned his customer inside. "I've arranged something special for our distinguished visitor from up north. The young lady will be most pleased to help you with whatever you might desire. All you need do is ask. Her name is Serita."

"And to what do I owe such extravagant attentions?" Longarm inquired.

Once again Smoot offered up another peculiar and toothy grin. "Well, sir, it appears that the recently departed Mr. Willy Coffin had a substantial amount of cash money on his person when you sent him to the Maker of all men for examination before the Golden Book and Final Judgment."

"Is that a fact?"

"Oh, most assuredly so. More than two hundred dollars in cold, hard coin, as a matter of pure, unadulterated truth. With those monies, plus the additional sale of his horse, tack, pistols, gun belt, rifle, and a few other odds and ends, the total of his earthly fortune provided me with a sum of nearly five hundred dollars."

"Nice payday, no doubt. But I guess I'm still not following your line of reasoning, Mr. Smoot."

"The lovely Serita is simply my way of saying thanks for delivering up a single customer that paid me nearly a year's wages, Marshal Long."

Custis Long smiled. "Most pleased to help out, Mr. Smoot."

"There is one thing about the lovely Serita you should be aware of, sir. She doesn't speak. Can't speak, to be completely accurate. Hasn't spoken since early childhood, as I understand. I think you'll find the experience most pleasurable." And with that, Smoot pulled the curtain closed and vanished.

As if by magic, a heavy-breasted, wide-hipped, and totally naked Mexican maiden of unmistakable beauty appeared from behind a curtain in the far wall. In a surge of sensual, feline motion, she jiggled to a spot beside a massive wooden vat of steaming, soapy water. Smiling, the remarkable Serita quickly stepped forward and took charge of Longarm's fresh change of clothing. She laid the neatly folded pile on a table in the corner opposite the tub, then rushed back and began pulling at his laces and buttons.

While he gladly encouraged the removal of all his dirty duds, Longarm stayed her hand when she touched the pistol belt strapped high on his waist. He pushed her away, removed the weapon himself, and placed it in an easy-to-access spot near the huge tub. Soon enough, though, the spirited señorita had the surprised lawman just as naked as she was.

Once they were both totally stitchless, the dark-eyed, raven-haired girl gently grasped his hand and led him to his already prepared and waiting bath. He gingerly stepped in and discovered that the water bordered on the skin-singeing.

Serita soundlessly giggled behind her hand at his contrived discomfort, but with very little effort got him immersed up to his armpits. With no further ado, she soaped a large rag, and went directly to the area between his legs.

After about a minute's worth of gentle, but insistent, encouragement, that eventually involved her sliding into the tub as well, the enthusiastic girl had Longarm's rigid manhood sparkling clean and stiffer than the barrel on a Sharp's Big .50 buffalo rifle.

"Good God, girl, you've gone and got the damned thing so hard a cat can't scratch it." He couldn't tell if she understood or not, but she again laughed without making any sound.

As he explored a pair of nipples that were harder than frozen acorns, she climbed aboard the object of all her previous attentions. For half an hour, or so, Serita gave Longarm a hot, slippery ride unlike anything he could have imagined available in an out-of-the-way place like Panther Mountain, Texas.

And while she said not a single word, the talented young woman nuzzled his ear and made barely audible, mewling, catlike sounds of pleasure he'd never heard come from any other woman before. The effect was nothing short of explosive.

Much too soon for his personal taste, Longarm kissed the girl good-bye and stepped back into Smoot's barber shop shaved, bathed, dried, pampered, and freshly dressed. He felt better than he had since a week before leaving Denver.

Smoot stood as though waiting on his most important customer. With a solicitous gesture, he opened the front door, and said, "Here, let me take all your soiled things. I'll have them cleaned and back to you by tomorrow afternoon at the very latest."

"You do know how to treat a patron, Mr. Smoot,

whether in this life, or in preparation for the next, I would imagine."

"Why thank you, sir. Most kind of you to say so."

"Bet if ole Willie Coffin could talk, he'd be more'n happy to say the same thing. Well, guess I'd best get back to the jail, or, better yet, maybe I'll stroll down the street to one of the saloons and get a bite to eat."

"Sounds like a capital idea, Marshal Long. Should you be in the vicinity of the Red Onion Saloon later this evening, I have already arranged a steak dinner with all the trimmings for you. And, please, feel free to order a bottle of their best liquor as well."

Longarm shook his head. "Mr. Smoot, you've done quite enough already. Serita was more than enough by way of thanking me. The meal isn't necessary."

"Oh, but I insist, sir. The actual cost to me is minimal when I consider the amount you so unselfishly provided me and my family from the pockets of the very dead Mr. Coffin. Please consider a plate of well-prepared victuals as my simple way of properly finishing up my thanks by providing a suitable end to your evening." Smoot extended his hand, and the men shook.

"Well, then, think I'll do as you advise," Longarm said and patted his rock-hard belly. "Seems like a fine evening for a stroll and, besides, I'm always ready for a steak dinner. Guess I'll head on down to the Red Onion. Short walk should give me a chance to see more of the town and perhaps meet a few of its citizens."

As Longarm turned and started down the dusty street, Smoot called out, "Do be careful, Marshal Long. While you've made a friend here, you mustn't forget that Hangtown Harry Moon still has allies of his own around as well. You've killed one and jailed two others, but there are still men right here in town that are not to be trusted in any instance. 'Specially when it comes to the disposition of your life."

For reasons he couldn't fully explain, something of the grave seemed to come through in the sound of Joshua Smoot's eerie wraithlike voice. Longarm shuddered in the fading light, brought his hand nearer the butt of his pistol, and paid closer attention to the dark and the lengthening shadows in Panther Mountain's doorways and alleys.

Chapter 10

Outside the Red Onion, celebrating tipplers spotted Longarm as he made his way down the street. Several cut their merriment short and ducked inside before he stepped onto the boardwalk. Others grew quiet, surreptitiously pointed, spoke in whispers, and moved aside as he ambled past them and stopped at the saloon's batwing doors. There's just nothing like an afternoon of unexpected slaughter to get people's undivided attention, he thought.

He lingered for several seconds on the knife-edge of light that fell from the busy cantina's interior and gazed inside. Like a number of other surprises in the dying town, the Panther Mountain oasis proved something of a startling oddity.

An immense bar that glistened in the soft light of numerous coal-oil lamps started just inside the swinging doors. The beautiful carved mahogany piece ran almost thirty feet down the entire wall to his left. A fully mirrored and well-stocked back bar covered either side of a massive, colorful, eye-catching painting. The twice-life-sized piece of artwork featured a totally unclothed and buxom blond beauty stretched out on her side in a most seductive pose.

All manner of whiskey, rye, and other liquors burdened the sparkling glass shelves and marble countertop. Rinky-tink music danced from a piano at the far end of the fancy drink-selling station. Longarm thought he recognized the tune, but couldn't be certain.

A solitary whiskey slinger cared for a mixed crowd of ten to twenty enthusiastic inebriates. Four coarse-featured women slithered from man to man and divided their attentions with those drinkers seated at one of the dozen or so tables scattered around the room. No dance floor or gambling accoutrement appeared in evidence on the ground floor. But a broad staircase, dead center in the back wall, very likely led upward to the heavenly bliss offered by games of chance.

Longarm caressed the grips of the big pistol mounted cross-draw fashion on his left hip. To make certain everything hung in just the right place, he lifted and resettled the pistol belt around his waist, then stepped inside.

He took up residence in an empty spot at the end of the counter near a polished-brass cash register. He liked the choice of location. Only a matter of steps back to the swinging door. But within a few seconds, Longarm realized that the beveled glass window facing the street exposed his back. So he moved farther into the corner to shield himself from any unpleasant surprises.

The bartender, a meatless, bald, tobacco-chewing creature, sported a handlebar mustache the size of an overland stage's singletree. Longarm's boot sole had barely hit the shined foot rail, when the liquor vendor spotted him, rushed over with a damp towel in hand, and wiped the already gleaming spot at the bar where he stood.

"Evenin', Marshal," he said and threw the rag over his skeletal shoulder. "Welcome to the Red Onion. Name's Everett Turner. Whatever your pleasure might be, it has already been taken care of. On the house, so to speak."

Longarm pulled a nickel cheroot from his vest pocket. Before he could get the cigar to his lips, a blazing lucifer flared in his face. "Don't usually light 'em," he said out of the corner of his mouth. "Been trying to quit for a number of years, you know. But tonight I do feel like a good smoke." Longarm sucked hard and then blew a gunmetal gray ring, the size of a number ten washtub, toward the ceiling. "Damn, but I do like the smell of these things."

The barkeep shook the match to death and dropped it into a waiting spittoon. "I would imagine the events of this afternoon warrant a good smoke, a drink, and a fine meal. As you can well imagine, everyone in town's talking. Been a spell since we've had anything like a stand-up shoot-out around these parts. Fact is, I can't even remember such a singular event a'tall. And I'd be willing to bet there ain't a living person in town over five years old that don't know your name because of what transpired out yonder in our street today."

"Well, Everett, you can tell any of those as might be interested, that I'd of preferred a much different outcome."

"I'll pass that along. Now then, how can I serve you, sir. Any particular liquor you favor, Marshal?"

"In fact there is, but I'd be heartily surprised if you had it available in your stock."

"You might well be shocked and amazed at what we at the Red Onion can provide, Marshal Long. Go right on ahead, try me."

"Usually drink beer, you know, but I do favor Maryland rye, when I can get it."

Turner's face lit up like a fourth of July whiz bang. "You're in luck, sir. Think I've got just what you want."

Seconds later Longarm watched as a double shot of fine Maryland rye flowed from a freshly opened bottle and sloshed into his glass.

"I'll leave the bottle," the smiling bartender said. "When you're ready, the table in the back corner is reserved especially for you, sir. My cook has his orders. Steak dinner's just waitin' for you to order it up."

Longarm saluted the bartender with his glass, threw down the double shot, then said, "Well, Everett, turn him loose. I like mine burned just enough to sear a good crust on it. Bloody inside, if you please."

"You take a seat, and I'll have 'er out to you in a matter of minutes, Marshal."

A good deal more relaxed than when he entered the place, Longarm carried his glass and bottle to the table, pulled out a chair, sat, tipped the wobbly seat back against the wall, and got comfortable. From his newly acquired perch, he could see nearly everything that transpired in the place. Men gathered in small groups around various tables, only to move to another spot if the mood struck them.

Painted women hopped from table to table, hugged the necks of first one man, then the next, and laughed at their crude jokes. Customers came and went, some joined friends at this or that table. Others entered, threw down one drink, and hurried away as quickly as they came.

After several minutes, Longarm relaxed even more and, at one point, caught himself on the verge of napping. Then Everett hustled over, carrying a plate that looked almost as big as a wagon wheel, and made quite a production of placing the feast on the table.

As Longarm's chair thumped back to the floor he said,

"Good God, Everett, that's one enormous big piece of beefsteak. Damned steer must've been about the size of a Concord coach."

The bartender beamed with unashamed pride. "Biggest damned steak you can get anywhere in Texas, by God. Along with taters, chuck wagon beans, sourdough biscuits, and such, it's one helluva meal. That pissant-sized chunk of gristle them folks serve at the Boar's Breath Saloon up in Amarillo cain't even compare."

Longarm grabbed a knife and fork and went to hacking at the meat. "I'll try to get her all down, but I'm not making any promises," he said, then shoved a chunk of the charred beef into his mouth.

"Eat however much you can, but be aware, there's still some of the best peach cobbler you've ever tasted a-waitin' when you're finished."

Halfway through the blanket-sized slab of perfectly grilled beef, Longarm had to admit defeat. He dropped both eating utensils onto the plate, rubbed and patted his stomach. Then, he forced up a magnificently satisfying belch just in time to notice nervous people across the room and near the bar start shifting aside, all fearful-like.

From under his hat brim, Longarm took note of a scar-faced, dead-eyed, sinister-looking gent, with greasy, shoulder-length hair. The man, got up in black from hat to boot, moved along the bar carrying a fresh tumbler of whiskey. The dangerous-looking gunny, armed with a double-holstered pistol rig that sported hand-sized, highly-polished silver conchos eased through the space provided by the saloon's still-scattering clientele. Bone-gripped Colt pistols sat high on each hip in hand-tooled, Mexican single-loop holsters, tilted at just the perfect angle for quick and death-dealing access.

Longarm slid farther down in his chair as though

about to nod off. He eased his weapon out, cocked and held the pistol in his lap under the table. Son of a bitch must be the Wagon Wheel's hired pistoleer, he thought, the man Walker Newman and Buster had warned him about. Longarm caressed the butt of the big .45, and waited.

Whiskey glass in hand, the man in black moseyed across the room and stopped a short distance from Custis Long's table. "Name's Braxton Pike, Marshal. You might'a heard of me. Sure as hell heard plenty about you today. Wonderin' if we could talk a spell?"

Longarm tilted his head back just enough to see Pike's face. Ice-blue eyes mounted in a blank, unreadable face stared back at him. "Don't think we've ever met, Mr. Pike. What exactly do we have to talk about?"

"There's always somethin', ain't they?" Pike said, as he reached out and placed one hand on the back of an empty chair across the table. "Mind if I set?"

Longarm nodded. "Suit yourself. It's a public house, Sit anywhere you like." He turned ever so slightly in his seat. Just enough to get his target back under the gun.

Braxton Pike flashed a toothy, crooked grin and settled into the creaking seat. With all the practiced delicacy of a grandmother at an afternoon Baptist tea party, he sipped his whiskey, then genteelly placed the glass on the table. The gunman wiped his fingers along each side of his moustache, and then carefully positioned both hands next to the drink in a gesture designed to put any itchy adversary at ease.

Longarm waited.

Pike smiled, squinted, and drilled the Denver-based lawman to his chair with an icy stare. "You can call me Brax, Marshal Long."

"Don't really know you that well. And I'm not all that

sure I want to find myself on a first name basis with a man of your reputation. Might have to drag you to justice, or kill you someday, Pike."

The gunfighter leaned forward, elbows, forearms, and hands on the table. "Well, then I'll get right to it. You caused quite a stir this afternoon, Marshal. Kilt Willy Coffin. Damn nigh blew the man in half, if the stories I hear are true."

"What you've said so far is close enough to raise a blister."

A reptilian grin split Pike's face. "Sure do wish I coulda seen that dance. Hell, everybody in town's talking 'bout the shooting—little kids all the way to Grandma. You'd think ever last one of these talky sons of bitches was there. Seen the whole damned thing. Personally wish I could have attended. Nothin' quite like the dance of death, is they? Unfortunately, I found myself occupied with other matters at the time."

"Willy called the tune, Pike. I gave the hard-headed son of a bitch several different opportunities to back away. Near as I've always been able to figure it though, any man stupid enough to go up against a shotgun, at close range, don't have any business using up other people's air."

"True enough, Marshal. And besides if you hadn't killed him I probably would have—sooner or later, anyway." Pike eased off his forearms a bit. "But I wouldn't have stopped with Willy. Him and them two other idiots hit town lookin' for any kind of trouble they could dish out. You had 'em all dead to rights. Shoulda took 'em all down—right then and there."

"Well, if either one of those other boys had gone for his weapon, Joshua Smoot would be a lot busier than he is right now."

Pike appeared to loosen up and assumed a thoughtful, almost philosophical demeanor. He leaned back with his elbows on the chair arms and stared at Longarm over peaked fingers. "Rumor has it, them fellers intended to brace me first chance they got, bein' as how I worked at the Wagon Wheel and Hangtown Harry worked over here, you see. Then again, maybe they just wanted to kill somebody—anybody. I was the only one in town with a reputation at the time. But then, you showed up and did me one helluva big favor, Marshal. When it all comes right down to it, just wanted to stroll over and thank you for a job well-done."

"Would say it was my pleasure, Pike, but I've never cared to rub a man out unless absolutely necessary."

"Way I heard-tell, Coffin gave you no damned lot of choice in the matter. And like you said, any man stupid enough to call a feller out, then draw down against a shotgun, don't need to go on living, as far as I can tell anyway."

Pike picked up his drink, slowly stood, and pushed his chair away from the table at the same time. "All I had to say. Except, maybe . . ."

"Go ahead, Pike, might as well get whatever's gnawing on you out in the open."

"Well, Marshal Long, just wanted you to know I ain't nearly as stupid as Willy Coffin. Should you and I ever have to go up against one another, believe me when I tell you, the outcome won't be as good for you."

Longarm used his free hand to pull a cheroot from his vest pocket. He held it between rock steady fingers and let his hand rest on the table where Pike could see it. "Guess you delivered your message, or threat, or whatever you want to call it. So, now, why don't you just run along? Let me enjoy my smoke in peace."

An evil, snaky grin squeezed Pike's lips together. "You know, Long, I can drop this glass and draw faster'n you can spit and holler howdy."

"You don't say?" Longarm growled.

"Oh, I do for damned sure say. You could be a dead man in a matter of seconds."

Longarm's pistol-filled hand slowly rose from its hiding place. He rested the barrel on the table's edge. The big .45's muzzle lined up on Pike's crotch. "Reckon you can draw faster than I can drop the hammer and blow your pecker and balls into a bloody wad in the floor behind you?"

Pike's smile widened. An almost perfect set of pearly white teeth sparkled, as he took a step backward, and said, "Slick. Real slick, Marshal. Sure didn't expect you to cover me before I even sat down. Well, guess I'll be movin' on out. There is just one other matter you might think on before I go."

A growing testiness crept into Longarm's voice when he said, "And just what in the hell might that be?"

"Well, you know, of course, that Moon's murderous brothers are on their way to Panther Mountain, right this very minute. Hell, they could ride up any time. Kill you, Marshal Byers, whole damned town, if'n they want to. Burn this entire pissant place right to the ground as well."

"Quit running me around the tree. Whatever you're trying to get at, Pike, go on and spit it out."

"Just that, being as how I don't have much use for Hangtown Harry, or any of the rest of his stupid family, for that matter, there's the very real possibility you might need my help on down the road a piece. Always good to have a friend who can use his guns, ain't it, Marshal?"

Longarm nodded. While his trust in Pike traveled no farther than he could throw a horse, he easily recognized an effort at a shaky truce when he heard it. "Mighty kind of you to make an offer like that, Brax. Should such an ugly necessity arise, I'll most certainly remember your offer."

Pike tipped his hat. "You do that, Marshal," he said. "And while you're at it, think once again on the undeniable fact that Shooter, Stump, and Axel Moon could be riding into town as we speak. Any one of them boys are as bad, or perhaps worse, than Hangtown Harry ever thought about being." Then, he turned and swaggered away.

The Red Onion's crowd loosened up and began to move about again, as soon as Pike hit the batwings and disappeared into the night. Longarm holstered his pistol and allowed the tension to drain into his boots. Laughter and movement all around the saloon returned, and a still-nervous piano player went back to his music.

Chapter 11

Everett Turner appeared at Longarm's elbow and motioned toward the Red Onion's still swinging doors. "Tell you true, Marshal, every time that son of a bitch comes in here, he scares the sulfurous hell out of my customers. Did you by any chance notice as how he looks like someone just dug him up out of a year-old grave? Ugly bastard gives me the bejabberous creeps."

Longarm scratched a match to life and lit the cheroot he'd been holding. As he shook the flame out, he said, "Proper response to the man, Mr. Turner. He's an extremely dangerous fellow—deadlier than Hangtown Harry ever thought about being. At least that's the opinion of some."

"Hell, everybody what patronizes the Onion knows that. Ain't to hard to see how afraid folks are of him. Situation is some odd though, when you think about it, Marshal."

"How so?"

"Well, have to admit he ain't hurt nobody around here yet—least ways not as I know of. Ain't even pulled one of them fancy pistols of his'n, so far. But, my glorious God, he is one scary son of a bitch. Walked up behind one of my regulars last week and the poor feller pissed hisself, standin' right over there at my bar. Made a helluva mess. Downright embarrassin', don't you think?"

Longarm motioned toward the seat Braxton Pike had recently vacated. "Why don't you sit a minute, Everett. I've got a little something on my mind we need to talk about."

Turner eagerly pulled the chair closer to Longarm, dropped into it, and said, "Hey, I'll help you out anyway I can. Whaddaya wanna know?"

"What's going on here that the Red Onion had Hangtown Harry on its payroll, and the Wagon Wheel felt compelled to hire a death-dealing skunk like Braxton Pike? The town seems peaceful enough—at least on the surface anyway."

Of a sudden, Everett Turner's manner changed, and he adopted a conspiratorial air. The drink-slinger glanced from side to side, around the room, and over his shoulder. He acted as though afraid someone unseen might be skulking nearby and hear whatever got said.

The skinny bartender trembled when he leaned to within inches of Longarm's face and almost whispered, "Mind you, while it ain't no big secret, and I suppose just about anyone could tell you the tale, it's probably best for me not to get caught talking about what happened. Sayin' the wrong thing to the law could have a deleterious effect on my health, if you get my drift."

Longarm thumped ashes from his cheroot onto the floor and jammed the smoke back into his mouth. Around the cigar he said, "Get on with whatever you've got to say, Everett. You can't know anything bad enough to make you afraid to tell it."

Turner's whisper got lower and more strained. "See,

up till 'bout a year ago, Panther Mountain was cookin' along right well. Then the absolute mortal realization hit every businessman in town that the rail line everyone'd counted on gettin' built simply wasn't a comin'. On top of that, and almost as bad, the telegraph that was supposed to have got stretched out this way got cancelled, too. Kinda left us high and dry, so to speak."

"Well, not having a telegraph office does make it a mite difficult to communicate with the outside world. You folks are pretty well isolated, way out here."

"Ain't that the damned truth? Lest you're on your way to Mexico or comin' back, ain't much reason to pass this way. And you mighta noticed as how a goodly number of businesses along Main Street have already closed down.

"Hard not to notice. First thing I saw coming in."

"Hell, we used to have four top-quality saloons operatin' full blast, seven days a week. The Palace, down the street, mighta been the finest drinkin' and gamblin' establishment this side of Fort Worth. All four of 'em stayed busy. Now there's only two."

"Your circumstances aren't all that unusual, Everett. Settlements like Panther Mountain come and go every day. Evidently this one got built on false promises and is now on its way down and out because those assurances didn't work the way everyone expected."

"Yeah, I suppose. Damned shame really. She'll likely be a ghost town in a few years. But there's people 'round these parts who ain't gonna let her die easy, Marshal. Competition for payin' customers in the saloon business has got right intense, here of late. Feller who owned this place, Potter Burton, well, he went and got hisself kilt 'bout six months ago."

"What happened?"

"Poor son of a bitch got rudely shot all to hell in the alley right out back of here one night after we closed. Buster Byers, that lazy stack of molderin' cow shit that goes for our town lawman, never did arrest nobody for the murder. That in spite of the glarin' fact that most folks were pretty sure they knew who done the bloody deed."

Longarm leaned closer to his informant and said, "And who do you and most other folks think killed Potter Burton, Everett?"

"Why that belly slinkin' scorpion, J. Butler Harrington, of course. Sweet sufferin' Jesus, ain't one shadow of a doubt far as me and anyone with any brains is concerned."

Longarm's eyebrows knotted up. He rubbed his forehead as though a crushing headache pounded behind his eyes. "Okay, I'll bite. Who exactly is J. Butler Harrington?"

"You ain't been payin' close attention have you, Marshal? Harrington's the sole proprietor and leadin' light of the Wagon Wheel Saloon, over yonder, 'cross the street. Employer of the deadly pistoleer, Braxton Pike. 'Course Harrington ain't been around much since Potter's unfortunate demise. He stays over in Fort Stockton, mostly. Let's Pike take care of the Wagon Wheel, near as any of us what ain't privy to the real going's on over there can tell."

Longarm nodded. "Ah. Now that does make your tale a lot clearer."

Turner waved as though to include anyone and everyone within miles of their table. "Whole town figures as how ole J.B. was simply tryin' to eliminate his only remainin' competition by murderin' off poor Burton."

"What did you mean when you said *trying*?"

"Well, seems J.B. went and misfigured just a mite."

"Misfigured? How so, Everett?"

"Burton's hot-tempered son, Jesse, come in and took over the Onion. Jesse's the one what sent for Hangtown

92

Harry Moon. Jesse said if'n Harrington, or anyone else, tried to kill him like got done for his pa, he wuz gonna make certain there was a harsh price paid by whoever got deemed responsible. Course, Jesse never had the where-withal to foresee as how Buster would end up a-whackin' Hangtown across the noggin and slappin' him in a jail cell. And, maybe even worse, he never anticipated J. Butler Harrington hirin' a killer like Braxton Pike to kinda take over the Wagon Wheel."

"You say Jesse Burton isn't here tonight?"

"Nope, but anytime he ain't at the saloon, you can bet he's down at the livery stable sniffin' around that hostler's daughter."

Longarm's eyes lit up. "Marley Newman?"

"Yep, that's the one. Bet it didn't take you ten minutes after you got to town to meet up with her. Steamin' little twitch, that 'un. Near as anyone 'round town can tell, 'at 'ere hot-assed gal cain't get enough of men, and just about any man'll do. Young Jesse spends an excessive amount of his wakin' hours with his nose stuck up a 'tween her long legs. And he's been known to get mighty rambunctious, if'n he finds out anyone else has been hangin' around that gal."

Longarm snorted. "Sounds like true love."

"Could be and then again maybe not. All I know for a true fact is that Jesse's blacked that gal's eye a time or two for real or perceived dalliances with other men around these parts. And he's threatened a killin' on more'n one occasion. Her and the other men."

"Like I said, sounds like true love to me."

Turner threw his head back, laughed, then said, "He is stuck on the girl. Bettin' money around town has it that if'n Marley Newman jumped off Panther Mountain's highest peak, it'd kill ole Jesse, too, bein' as how his head is wedged so far up her ass. Can tell you, without reservation, that everyone workin' here at the Onion is glad when he's gone and pesterin' the hell out of her 'stead of botherin' us. Boy's got about as much in the way of business smarts as a wagonload of rocks. More time he spends away from here the better. Fact is, with J. Butler a-livin' in Fort Stockton and Jesse out of pocket most times, been pretty quiet 'cept for when Buster clubbed the shit out of Hangtown Harry."

"Get the impression from the way you talk, Jesse's not too smart, huh?"

"Swear to Jesus he's just like a catfish, Marshal, all mouth, no brains. Poor dumb bastard has the power to piss off the average person simply by openin' that bucket hole of his'n and speakin'."

"Sounds like young Mr. Burton isn't the best loved of Panther Mountain's leading citizens."

Turner cupped a hand over his mouth and whispered, "Now there's an understatement if they ever wuz one. Hateful little shit is roundly disliked by just about everyone that's ever had any dealin's with 'im."

"Why's that?"

"His pa, ole Potter Burton, was about as likable a feller as you'd ever come across. Bet you cain't find anybody 'round these parts what didn't profess a fondness for the man. But his sorry son is exactly the opposite. Boy's a real hard case. Meaner'n a bulldog on a gunpowder diet. Thinks he's John Wesley by God Hardin, or maybe Wild Bill, for Christ's sake—some think he's not only stupid, but crazy on top of it."

"Bad combination, if I ever heard one described, Everett."

"Marshal, I do believe he'd use his own nose to pick a fight with a diamondback rattler. Somethin' in the boy's

94

thinker box, number of the cogs, wheels or such, just ain't exactly tied to the rod that runs the rest of his buggered up brain. On top of everything else he travels in the company of a pair of dangerous semi-idiots named Tubbs. Claude and Eli Tubbs. Folks hereabouts have a nickname for Claude. They calls 'im Booger."

Longarm grinned, took a draw on the cheroot, then said, "Booger, huh? Sounds like a bad one."

"All three of 'em is crazy and bad. Eli's the smart one, but don't say much. Booger, he's like Jesse, runs his mouth like a Gatlin' gun, but he's just about smart 'nuff to screw up an anvil with a rubber hammer."

Longarm shook his head and grinned again. "Promise I'll watch out for them, Everett. I'm genuinely grateful for your expressions of concern and the warning. One question though. If Jesse had men like Eli and Booger around, why'd he need Hangtown Harry Moon as well?"

"Eli and Booger ain't nothin' more'n town trash. They'll beat the bejabberous hell out of a feller for little or nothin', but I don't know of anyone as they've kilt yet, least ways not around these parts. Hangtown Harry, on the other hand, is an authentic, dyed-in-the-wool man-killer. I've always thought that Jesse had something special in mind for Harrington. They's some as believe that's why Harrington lit out. Others say Jesse just ain't got around to killin' Harrington yet, but he will."

Turner stood, appeared ready to leave, but toed the sawdust-covered floor. His gaze darted around the room as though looking for ghosts behind every chair. "Guess maybe I've done run my mouth just about enough," he said. "Pretty sure Jesse would deal me a wagon load of shitty misery, if'n he found out I been talkin' 'bout 'im."

"All sounded like fairly common knowledge to me, Everett."

95

"Yeah, well, don't matter one whit if what I done said be true or not. Never know how he'll react if'n he finds out we talked like this. You just ain't got no idea how far off his bubble is from bein' plumb."

"Well, he won't hear anything of our discussion from me."

"See here, Marshal, I don't mean to sound like I'm pryin', but you look done in. Probably wouldn't be a bad idea to get some rest. Would appear to me you've had a long, tough day, what with just gettin' here, the shootin', Willy Coffin's demise, and Braxton Pike's visit."

Longarm stood and pushed his chair away. "You're dead on right, Everett. Think maybe I'll stroll on back down to the jail. Get some sleep."

"Want me to wrap up what's left of your steak? Bet Mr. Smoot would want you to have it. Make you a damned fine breakfast come tomorrow morning. Good piece of steak, rest of them taters, and a fresh cup of coffee can really get a man going."

"That'd be much appreciated, Everett." Longarm slapped the bartender on the shoulder. "Much appreciated."

Chapter 12

Longarm pushed through the Red Onion's batwing doors and stepped onto the dusty, poorly lit, creaking board-walk. He crawfished his way out of the single shaft of available light that fell from inside the saloon, placed his package of leftover steak, wrapped and tied in butcher's paper, under his arm, and pulled a cheroot from his vest pocket. After a long pause, he shoved the cigar between clenched teeth—unlit.

Dark and virtually deserted, Panther Mountain's main thoroughfare no longer entertained small knots of drunken revelers, left over from the afternoon's deadly events. Low-hanging, rust-colored clouds covered an inky sky bereft of stars. Blood-tinged moonlight deep-ened the ominous gloom, and cast menacing shadows from every business entrance, water trough, and possible assassin's hiding place.

Longarm carefully eyeballed each nook and cranny for concealed threats. He shrugged as chicken flesh ran up his sweaty spine. Perfect night for another killing, he thought.

With practiced caution, Longarm turned and started

back for Buster Byers's office and the much desired safety and security of a soft, comfortable place to sleep. For a fleeting moment, the image of Marley Newman, buck-assed nekkid on her back and beckoning, flashed across his fevered mind, but he immediately dismissed the thought and focused on the prospect of dry gulching weasels waiting in the dark. Years of past experience forced him to hesitate before each building's entry. He gave watchful attention to alleyways before exposing himself to the likelihood of potential ambush.

He keyed the padlock on the jailhouse door and had just breathed a sigh of pleased relief when a rush of movement from the darkness swarmed around him. Just over the threshold, Everett Turner's carefully trussed package hit the floor with a resounding thump. The surprised lawman's pistol came out and up in a flash as he grappled with his assailant.

His free hand landed on, then squeezed a melon-sized breast. In the inky darkness, the woman attached moaned like a cougar in heat.

"Jesus girl," he snapped, "I damned near shot you deader than hell in a preacher's front parlor."

Lips found his neck, cheek, then greedily covered his mouth. An incredibly long, flaming hot tongue forced his teeth apart and filled his mouth.

She broke the kiss, grabbed at the fingers rolling her flint-hard nipple, forced them up under her loosened skirt and slapped them between her widely straddled legs. Sucking air like she'd just run a mile, his still-unseen aggressor grunted, "I've been waitin' for this ever since you rode into town. You're just about the best-lookin' hunk of man I've ever seen. Ain't nothin' around this nowhere, do-nothin' berg that even compares."

Longarm holstered his pistol, helped the girl massage

her dripping sex, then led both of them inside the jail-house. He pushed the door closed with his foot. "You know, Miss Marley," he said, "way I hear it, Jesse Burton just might not approve of such behavior on the part of his loving sweetheart."

For about a second, Marley Newman stiffened under his insistent caresses, leaned away, and pulled her hand free; then she went back on the attack with a vengeance. Her tongue moistened his ear as much as he'd moistened her overheated woman's flesh.

"How'd you find out about Jesse?" she breathed into Longarm's now dripping ear.

"Hell, girl, don't guess it really matters right this very minute, does it?" he said.

The hot-blooded female rubbed her nipples across his chest, slipped one hand down to his crotch, and whimpered, "Well, that tiny-dicked, vicious little shit ain't here right now is he?" She cupped his crotch and squeezed. "On the other hand . . ." Her talented fingertips, coaxed, stroked, and quickly pulled him into a state of rigidity similar to a heat-hardened railroad spike.

"Come on, gimme some!" she hissed.

Using his thumb and forefinger, Longarm found the perfect spot at the volcanic juncture between Marley Newman's silky thighs and stroked. The randy girl growled, lept into the air, and encircled his waist with long, muscular thighs. Her leather skirt rode all the way up to her waist.

Longarm staggered, balanced himself, then ran his free hand down her back, fumbled beneath the thin folds of soft leather. He cupped and squeezed a naked ass shaped and hardened by years of riding bareback around West Texas like a Comanche Indian. The girl snorted with unbridled lust, smeared her molten sex up, down, around, and all over the front of his pants to the point where she unexpectedly shuddered in his arms, then whimpered like a small child, and rested her forehead on his shoulder.

For about five seconds, Longarm thought perhaps the lustful Marley had prematurely brought the encounter to a surprising and unplanned consummation. He couldn't have been more wrong.

Of a sudden, the girl came back to life like someone had jabbed her rock-hard, shapely ass with a red-hot pitch fork. Insistent hands darted between them again as she groped with the buckle of his pistol belt. In short order, the heavy weapon fell to the floor with a resounding thud. She clawed and grappled with the buttons until his pants dropped, only to hover around his knees.

The gasping woman grabbed him about the neck with one arm, pulled herself upward, as high as she could, and then abruptly slid down and onto his one-eyed trouser snake with an animalistic grunt. She shouted, threw her arms up and out, and rode him with all the unbridled abandon of a cowgirl eager to stay on an unbroken mustang. Each buck and bounce drove Longarm even deeper still.

"Hot damn," she squealed.

Holding on to her wondrously active behind for dear life, Longarm shuffled across the pitch-dark office, toward the spot where he figured the bed had to be located. Consumed in the single-minded twin efforts of trying to satisfy the bucking girl, and, at the same time, find the lumpy cot, he banged his shins on the wooden bedframe. His pants, now gathered round his feet, tripped him, and the two of them pitched sideways. They ended up flopping around on the floor like beached, but permanently connected fish.

He pushed himself up on his hands and knees, and continued to piston his hips into the wildly thrashing woman beneath. "Wait. Wait," he said in an effort to try and slow the action.

She slapped him on the upper arm so hard it sounded like a pistol shot. "No! No! Don't you dare stop!" Then, she grabbed his head and pulled it down to her heaving breasts. "Sweet Jesus, keep it going! Keep it going! More! More! Harder! Harder!"

He sucked on one nipple, then the other, tugging like a newborn babe. Longarm raised his head and gasped, "But it'll be a lot more comfortable in the bed, won't it?"

"The hell with the bed, just don't stop," she yelped.

"Jesus, girl, we keep rolling around on the floor like this . . . we're gonna end up with our elbows, knees . . . and such . . . all full of wood splinters."

Marley Newman let out a gasping hoot and brought her hips up so hard she almost bucked him off. "Hell, I've already got a big ole *splinter* the size of a hatchet handle inside me now." She shoved her hips high and held him there. "Little bitty piece of wood here and there ain't gonna mean nothin?"

From inside the cell block Hangtown Harry Moon yelled, "Oh for the sweet love of God. Have mercy on us poor prisoners. We can hear ever damned thang y'all is a-doin' out there, Marshal. For Christ's sake, you could at least try to be a little quieter. Listenin' to y'all ain't nuthin' but sheer torture. I ain't had no cooz myself since a week before Buster locked me up in this goddamned place. Have to sit in here, horny as hell, a-polishin' my own knob, for cryin' out loud. Kinda thang could drive a man to the precipice of total blindness."

Marley Newman giggled, then yelled back, "Quit whining for Christ's sake. I cain't concentrate on what I'm doing out here if I have to spend any time laughin' at you nimrods."

Longarm let out a hearty guffaw at her brazen boldness. "Good Lord Almighty, but you are one bad, bad girl."

She pulled his head back down onto her sweaty breasts, stuck her tongue in his ear again, and licked him to a state of near delirium. Pulled his head back and held it between her hands. "Yeah, I'm bad all right," she hissed. "Not one single doubt about it. But you like me that way, don't you, big fella? All you men like me, when I'm down and dirty, hot and nasty. The nastier the better. Go on, tell me it ain't true. Tell me how you'd rather I was a blond-haired saint that wouldn't let you touch me."

"Can't," he groaned.

"Aw, go on, tell me how you'd rather do it with a sweet little blue-eyed, Bible-thumpin' virgin who'd lay there and squeak like a church mouse."

"Told you already, I can't."

Despite everything he tried, in a concentrated effort to keep the absolute inevitable from happening, Longarm's spine suddenly kinked up like a rusted logging chain, went rigid, and snapped into immovable place, link by link, accompanied by a reverberating grunt. Driving hips plunged downward like a sledge-hammered drill bit and nailed Marley Newman to the floor as he spewed his entire being into her gushing, receptive body.

A minute or so later, he rolled onto his sweaty back and lay spent and motionless beside her. In the dark she said, "Sweet Merciful Father, I ain't ever had a ride like that. God, I'm still comin'. Damn. Bet if we had a lamp lit I could see smoke rolling off my quiverin' notch. God, but I knew you were gonna be a good 'un, Long. Feel like my whole body might just bust into flame."

After an extended yawn, Longarm said, "Well, whatever of yours might, or might not, be smoking, or shooting sparks and flares to the ceiling for that matter, you're gonna have to take yourself home and let it burn itself out there. I've got to get some sleep. Have no idea what might be coming my way tomorrow. Can't be functioning at half-speed."

He felt the girl sit up beside him, and heard a muffled scramble of movements as she groped around on the floor searching for the various garments they'd cast aside during their initial tussle. After some minutes of hunting and scrounging and getting redressed, she said, "Hell's bells, I never intended on stayin' all night anyway."

Then he felt her hand on him again. Before he could even think to react she fell to licking, kissing, and sucking on his semirigid tool like tomorrow would never come. An anguished groan oozed out of him as he slid his fingers into her hair and pulled her enthusiastic lips and tongue away from their ardent devotions. Her mouth found his in the dark, and then she was on her feet in a flash and out the door.

As she pulled the heavy panel closed behind her, she said, "Given any opportunity at all, I'll be back for another one of these treatments, just as soon as humanly possible, Marshal Long. Best be thinkin' ahead, 'cause there's a very real possibility that things could actually get wild next time around."

The door slammed shut. Longarm crawled to the bed and clambered in. The image of a naked, sweaty, Marley Newman sitting astride him, whooping like a wild Indian, with a riding crop in one hand and a Boss of the Plains hat in the other flashed across the backs of his eyes. Jesus, he thought, she reminds me of Tildy Potter.

In the pitch-black cell block, Hangtown Harry Moon called out, "Thank God she finally left. Maybe now we can all get some fuckin' sleep."

Chapter 13

Next morning, a scorching sun boiled up from the east and oozed onto the streets of Panther Mountain like volcanic lava. Longarm groaned when the harsh light from one window finally crept far enough across the floor to slap him in the corner of his eye like a hot barber's towel.

A second later Armondo Diez, grinning, bowing, and sweating, brought in the morning's breakfast of tortillas, meat, refried beans, and a variety of freshly shredded vegetables for the prisoners. The beaming Mexican barefooted his way across the marshal's office, headed right for the jailhouse ring of heavy brass keys, and let himself inside the cell block.

Soon as Hangtown Harry Moon saw Diez, he groaned so loud passersby on the street should have heard him as clearly as Longarm. "Aw shit," Moon grumped, "our first dose of Messican ass-burners is here, boys."

Charlie Tatum said, "Why don't yew give 'er a rest, Harry. This little feller's food ain't half bad. Personally, I like them tor-tillers. 'Specially these here flour kind Armondo's been a bringin' us. Smear some beans on one of 'em, slap on some of that fried meat and a pile of his veg-etables, and yew done got yerself a whole meal."

"Yeah," offered Whitey Kilgore. "Why doncha just quit yer grippin', Harry. I'm hungry enough to eat the ass end out of a dead armadiller. These here Messican beans, and such, is mighty damned good, if'n yuh ask me. Sure as hell beats sittin' 'round starvin'."

"Well, nobody asked either of you idiots how you feel about a damned thing," Moon snapped. "You're supposed to of got me outta this fuckin' hellhole, but look at 'cha. Messed around and got a good gun hand like Willy Coffin kilt deader'n Davy Crockett. Now you're locked up and eatin' fart berries, same as me. Lotta damned good either one of you is."

Longarm wrapped the lower half of his naked body in one of Marshal Byers's scratchy blankets, rummaged around in his pile of belongings, found a full bottle of rye in the saddlebags, then stiff-legged his way over to the washstand in the corner behind the local lawman's desk.

He glared at the image staring back from the cracked and stained mirror. "Sweet mother of God," he groaned to himself, "slept like a dead man, and the damned bed seemed comfortable, but it sure as hell knotted me up like a bad piece of hemp."

He sloshed a mouthful of the potent liquor around his furry-feeling mouth, swallowed, then poured water into the basin from a badly nicked jug and mixed in a cupful of the liquor. A ragged chunk of cloth snatched from a peg beside the mirror and dipped in the tepid liquid was used to scrub himself pink from his waist to his hairline in a quick, but thorough, El Paso whorehouse bath. The cold-water scrubbing blasted the remaining mattress lint from Longarm's sleep-numbed brain and brought a fresh twinkle and sharpness to his wide-set, gunmetal-blue eyes.

He pulled on a fresh, gray shirt from his possibles bag, cinched up the hated shoestring tie now required by the bureaucrats in Washington, donned his favorite vest, and then fought his way into a fresh pair of cotton long johns and clean tweed pants. He cursed and grumbled until the stovepipe, knee-high, cavalry boots finally felt comfortable on his feet, then stepped out onto the jailhouse's little covered porch for a glance up and down the street.

Longarm's steely gaze raked the entire length of Panther Mountain's central thoroughfare, then fell on a shirt-tailed kid of about twelve or thirteen standing on the steps of the jail's porch with a chewed-up sombrero in his hands. "Your name, Jesus Sanchez?" he said.

"*Sí*, señor, I am Jesus Sanchez."

"You speak English. *¿Habla usted ingles, Jesus?*"

"My English is very good, Señor Marshal."

Longarm pulled a fresh cheroot from his vest pocket and lit it. "You hungry, Jesus?"

"*Sí*, señor. Jesus always hungry."

"Well, come on in. Senor Diaz is in the cell block feeding the prisoners. Should be plenty enough for you to have some as well."

"No, señor. Jesus does not eat until his work is finished. He must empty the prisoner's chamber pots, sweep out the office, and wipe away as much dust as possible. Marshal Byers requires these labors in return for my food. But the past few days he has locked me out. I am behind in my efforts."

Longarm blew smoke from the corner of his mouth, then said, "I admire your work ethic, son. You come on in and do your job as usual. I'll have Armondo leave your meal on the desk, and you can eat whenever you feel the urge. How's that sound to you?"

"*Es muy amable, señor.*"

The boy made a motion with one hand and whispered something Longarm couldn't hear. A mottled yellow and black dog, the size of a small pony, dragged itself from under the porch beneath the astonished marshal's feet and shook itself all over. Dust and trash flew off the beast in a thick, rolling cloud.

"Diablo comes, too, Marshal. He watches the prisoners for me while I open their cells."

Longarm snorted, "The dog guards them while you work in their cells?"

"*Sí*, señor. Even bad men like *Señor* Moon would not dare to anger, Diablo."

"Diablo? You named your dog the Devil?"

A blinding smile flashed across the boy's dark face as he scratched behind his pet's ears. "Yes. He is a devil, but a good one. He protects Jesus. Were it not for Diablo," he patted the dog's grizzly-sized head, "Jesus Sanchez would have been dead many times over, señor."

The gigantic animal turned and gazed up at Longarm like a wolf examining a lean and tasty piece of beefsteak. A wide, thick, dark pink tongue rolled out of the dog's mouth as he puffed and sniffed the lawman's scent into his wet, black snout. It licked at a blood-red muzzle and slurped. Flat, bronze-colored eyes blinked slowly as though to send the lawman the message that, "Hey, I'm not afraid of a damned thing on this earth. Especially you, you long, thin son of a bitch."

Longarm stepped out of the doorway and motioned the boy and dog inside. Jesus disappeared over the threshold, but his furry, dangerous-looking friend stopped and, for what seemed like an eternity, snuffled around the lawman's booted feet. The uneasy marshal casually brought his hand to the butt of his pistol. He tried not to act unduly alarmed by the monster's slobbering examination. The beast's gaze lazily moved upward, and the two stared into each other's eyes once again. Longarm couldn't believe it, but the creature appeared to smile, then when Jesus called out for him, Diablo casually ambled off into the jail.

The curious marshal followed the boy and his hairy friend back inside. He leaned against the doorframe and watched with considerable curiosity as Jesus took the keys from their peg, and strode into the cell block like an old and experienced lawman checking on his incarcerated wards. The dog pricked its ears, and followed.

"Señor Moon. ¿Cómo está usted?"

Moon hopped off his bunk and moved back against the wall. "You know full goddamned well, I doan speak no Messican of any kind, boy. Been tellin' you ever since I got put in this stink hole."

"Ah, yes, so you say, señor. It does not matter. You know why I am here, do you not?" As though to punctuate what the boy said, a low, ominous rumble emanated from somewhere deep inside the dog's thick chest. The brute's lips peeled away from its muzzle revealing thick, sharp canine teeth.

Harry Moon blanched and pressed himself flatter against the wall. He appeared as though glued there. "Hell, yes. I know why you're here. Been sleepin' in this dump long enough to know who you are and what you do. 'Sides, your goddamned mutt already bit me once. Good thing I had my boot on at the time, or I'd probably still be nursing a severe puncture wound." Moon shook a trembling finger at the boy. "Just you make sure you keep that big son of a bitch dog away from me. You hear? Don't you dare let him inside my cell."

Trembling like a windblown leaf in late fall, Moon grabbed up his chamber pot by its wire handle, carefully placed it on the floor by the door, and crawfished back to his spot against the far wall. He waved at his inquisitive friends without taking his eyes off the still-growling animal and said, "You boys best do the same. The kid has a job to do. Might as well let him get his chores done and over. Besides, it stinks to high heaven in here after an entire afternoon and night of you bastards gettin' rid of all them beans Armondo's been a-bringin' that y'all both seem to love so damned much."

Charlie Tatum scratched his stubble-covered chin, grinned, revealing yellowed, crooked teeth, then said, "Yew a-skeered of this Messican kid's little ole puppy dog there, Harry?"

Moon's twisted, sneering face jerked around Tatum's direction. "Yeah, Charlie. Damned right. Don't mind sayin' it, neither. I'm a-skeered of the damned dog. You should be as well. Near as I can tell, the hair-covered bastard came straight from Hell itself and given any opportunity, he'll take a chunk out of your poor dumb ass. Damned animal's a man-killer just as sure as Hell's hot."

Straddle-legged, head jutted forward, neck stretched in attack stance, Diablo stood beside Jesus as the boy ran the key into the lock and snapped open the barred door like an experienced jailer. Still smiling, he leaned inside, retrieved the sloshing object of his efforts, and locked Hangtown Harry back in. Moon stayed pressed against his cell's back wall until he heard the metallic click that insured his continued captivity—and safety.

Jesus deposited the smelly container next to the jail's thick back door for transportation to the outhouse. The same careful practiced process took place with Charlie Tatum, too. Everything appeared to have gone well and continued to do so, leastways, until the boy got to Whitey Kilgore.

Kilgore, who'd never been celebrated as a man of vast, or even limited, intelligence, had napped through breakfast and Harry Moon's fearful recitation of his encounter with Diablo. But the sleeping gunman popped awake, as though taken completely by surprise, and rolled off his cot when the cell door clanked opened. He appeared to make a threatening move toward Jesus—a blindingly stupid, unthinking mistake. In the blink of an eye, the boy's snarling guardian lunged, and struck Kilgore in the chest with both front feet. An instant later the dog had the stunned and frightened prisoner flat on his back. The growling animal loomed over the frozen jailbird. Huge droplets of slobber dripped on the trembling man's bared neck.

In a soft voice, Jesus said, "No. No. No. Come, *mi amigo. Es nada. Nada.* He didn't mean anything. Come, Diablo. Come away." Jesus's devil actually wagged a frayed tail, then shook its massive head, slinging dog spit all over Kilgore's face, the bunk, and the cell at large.

Longarm smiled and pushed himself away from the door frame. He strode to the boy's side and placed a hand on his shoulder. "Tell you what, Jesus. Given what I've just seen, I'm gonna leave you in charge of the jail while I stroll down the street to Josh Smoot's place and get a shave. I have complete faith you'll make certain these men behave while I'm gone. How's that sound?"

The boy actually appeared to light up inside. He threw Longarm a beaming smile and said, "You needn't fear, señor. I will leave Diablo here between the cells to guard the prisoners. They won't do anything while my good friend watches."

111

"No. No, I don't think they will," Longarm said and glanced around at the still shocked trio of outlaws.

As the grinning deputy marshal started for the outer office, he heard Jesus saying, "Outside. You can come outside *ahora*, Diablo. *Es bueno*. Everything *es bueno, mi amigo*."

Chapter 14

Joshua Smoot had, once again, performed magic with his wickedly sharp, ivory-handled straight razor. Covered with a spotlessly clean sheet, Custis Long reclined in Smoot's adjustable, leather-covered, hair-cutting throne, and hovered on the contented edge of going back to sleep. A steaming towel, draped around his shaved face, had for the second time in two days achieved a level of silky smoothness similar to that found only on a three-day-old baby's ass.

The dozing lawdog luxuriated in that between-world of semiconsciousness and total relaxation a man could usually only find while seated in a skilled barber's chair. The soothing odors of a variety of hair tonics, lotions, soaps, bay rum, witch hazel, and other such manly-smelling colognes, combined with the heavy aroma of to-bacco in all its sundry forms, and the specialized skills of a talented man with a razor had the power to soothe even the most agitated mind.

But just as Longarm was about to drift off into forty comfortable winks for real, a rush of noise and move-ment filled the shop. The door burst open. He heard the silver bell attached to the portal's header that announced entering customers almost jingle out of its anchor in the frame. Heard the footfalls of at least three men, as they clomped into the room dragging a variety of jingling spurs attached to heavy boots. Heard the door forcefully slam shut.

Longarm shifted ever so slightly in the chair. Unseen beneath the sheet, his fingers slipped around the oiled-walnut grips of the pistol laid in his lap. He leveled the muzzle in the direction of the noise for ready use and waited.

From behind him Longarm heard Smoot say, "Mornin', Jesse. You needin' a shave, or maybe a haircut today? Throw in a right fine rolling cream massage, if'n you've got the time and inclination. How 'bout you Claude, Eli?" The man's voice had changed. An almost undetectable tremor tinted some of his words. He sounded more than a bit unnerved. A hot prickly sensation of anticipation crept down Longarm's spine, trickled along his arm, and settled in the relaxed grip on the pistol's butt.

Someone said, "Pull that goddamned towel off'n the woman-stealin' bastard's face, Josh. I aim to have words with 'im. Want to look the squirrley son of a bitch in the face 'fore I put a couple of holes in his worthless hide."

Someone else muttered, "Yeah, we're gonna have some words with the woman-stealin' bastard, then put some holes in his worthless hide."

In one well-practiced motion, Panther Mountain's combination furniture maker/undertaker/barber/preacher/veterinarian whipped the steaming towel off his only customer's face, and, in the same motion, expertly elevated the chair while turning it slightly toward the quarrelsome speakers.

Longarm blinked, pinched the bridge of his nose with his free hand, and squinted until the man directly in front of him came into sharp focus. Barely five feet seven inches tall, rail thin, and ferret-faced, Jesse Burton packed a pair of bone-gripped Colt pistols strapped high on his waist behind a fancy red sash. Their carved grips peeked from a butts first, Wild Bill Hickok, gunfighter's position.

Stoop-shouldered and red-faced, Burton sneered at Deputy U.S. Marshal Custis Long from beneath a palm-leaf sombrero that sported an extravagant concho-decorated, horsehair band. The hat resembled a small tent sitting atop his head. On either side of the Red Onion's red-faced, quivering owner stood two burly, gun-toting toadies who looked to Longarm as though they could easily eat handsaws and spit roofing tacks.

Jesse Burton threw his head back, peered down his nose and said, "You're that marshal from Denver, ain't you? One they call Longarm? Feller who shotgunned Willy Coffin out yonder in the street 'tother day."

"Guess you done gone and caught me, mister. I'm the very one alright. What's on your mind?"

"Hear you've been messin' round with my woman, you son of a bitch."

Longarm recalibrated the spot where he wanted his first shot to hit and said, "First of all, I don't think we've ever met. And, second of all, you're interrupting the closest thing to a religious experience that I'm accustomed to having in any given week, mister. My daily shave is real important to me. Don't like to be bothered until after I'm finished."

Burton punched the gunny on his right, snorted, and said, "Well, you can just get on up outta that chair, step right on over here, and kiss my pimply, hair-covered ass if you think for a single instant I give a hoot in Hell whether I'm a-*botherin'* you or not. Came here to talk about you molestin' my woman, you lanky stack of skunk shit."

"Just who in the hell are you? And what woman is it I'm supposed to have molested?" Longarm knew the answer to both questions, but wanted to see just how much he could actually irritate the puffed up little saloon owner before bringing the silly dance to an abrupt halt.

Burton's face flushed. He shook a dirty-nailed finger at Longarm and snapped, "You know good and goddamned well who I am. Name's Jesse Burton. I own the Red Onion Saloon down the street. Marley Newman's my woman, by God, and there ain't a man under sixty years old, within fifty miles, what don't know it."

With his free hand, Longarm motioned for Smoot to bring the barber chair completely upright. Once comfortable again, he said, "Suppose it best for you to get to the back of your place and out of the way of any potential gunfire, Josh. Mr. Burton appears determined to cause trouble this morning."

Smoot threw everyone in the room a nervous nod, said, "Yes, sir. Think I'll do just that." An instant later he vanished through the shop's back door.

A broken-nosed, scar-faced, thick-necked escapee from one of Hell's deepest circles stood beside Burton and growled, "You know, Jesse, bet I could snap this here feller's neck like a rotten twig. All you gotta do is say the word and I'll get a-hold of his feet and mop this hair-covered floor up with the prissy bastard's freshly-clipped mustache."

Burton let a derisive snort of laughter escape at the troll's feeble joke. He slapped his smart-mouthed crony on the shoulder and said, "Well, now that might be right hard to do, Booger. Heard-tell this 'un here's a bad, bad, real bad man. Done kilt Willy Coffin, right out yonder in the street, and ain't even been in town but one day."

Claude Tubbs contemptuously spat. "Son of a bitch don't look so damned tough to me 'thout a shotgun in his hands, Jesse. 'Sides, I ain't seen him kill nobody myself. Could be nothin' more'n a wild tale folks 'round here done made up, or somethin'. Bet he ain't got no more bark on his tender ass than a creek-huggin', weepin' willer tree. You tell me when, and I'll shuck him out like an ear of farm-growed, ripe Iowa corn."

From out of nowhere came the voice of reason. Eli Tubbs said, "I don't like this, Jesse. Don't like it a'tall to tell the righteous truth. Let's just back outta here and let this 'un go."

Burton's angry-faced grin fell for about a second, but he recovered and shot back, "Hell, no. I come here to kill this badge-wearin' weasel. Or, at the rock-bottomed least, let you boys stomp a ditch in him, and then stomp 'er dry as a West Texas arroyo in August."

"Damned right," Claude Booger Tubbs said. "Any man who'd maliciously fuck another man's woman, at the very by God least, needs to have his ears tied in a bow knot somewhere on the backside of his dumb-assed head."

Longarm had heard about all he wanted to hear. He groaned, squirmed in the chair, and said, "I'm generally a patient man, Burton. Usually I'd sit here and listen to this go on for at least another minute, or maybe even two. But you boys have worn your welcome completely out this morning. Interrupted my shave. Called me names, even accused me of something I didn't do. So, I think it's time for all three of you to hit the street back to the Red Onion, or wherever you usually waste your time on a day like today. And don't let Josh Smoot's door hit you in the ass on the way out."

Booger Tubbs threw his head back and cackled like a crazed rooster. Then, he hooked his thumbs over his pistol belt and got all serious-faced. He zeroed in on Longarm and snarled, "We'll leave when Jesse says we're done. Or, even better yet for me, you can drag your sorry ass up outta 'at 'ere chair, come on over here and make us leave?"

Longarm snatched the sheet away to reveal the Frontier model Colt leveled at Jesse Burton's guts. "I asked you boys to hit the street about as nice as I know how to do it, given the circumstances. Now I'm telling you. Keep your hands where I can see them, get yourselves out of my face, and head on back to the Red Onion, before I lose what's left of my rapidly dwindling temper."

Jesse Burton shook like a man in the final throes of a yellow fever attack. "You gonna deny that you've done been diddlin' my woman?"

Longarm feigned shock and surprise. He saw no reason to kill the man over such a trivial matter. "Where did you hear such a thing, Jesse?"

"Marley told me herself, by God. Hell, she's tellin' everyone in town as how you done went and took unwanted advantage of her."

Infuriated, Longarm flicked the pistol muzzle in the general direction of the shop's door again. "I don't believe a word of what you just said. Find it difficult, to the point of impossible, to credit any young woman with bringing unwanted attention on herself in such a way."

Burton swelled up like a swap-dwelling bullfrog. "Well, I don't personally give a rat's ass what you believe, mister."

Longarm blanched and snapped, "I've never forced any woman to do a damned thing she didn't want to do in my entire life. Besides, whatever might or might not have happened between Marley Newman and me, if anything did, is strictly between her and me. Now, get the hell out of here, before you push me right over the edge, boy. I'm sick of listening to this unneeded ration of steaming horseshit."

Fully chastened, and searching for an easy exit, Booger and Eli Tubbs carefully backed away from the angered lawman, and heeled it for the street, but Burton wouldn't let up. "You're gonna go and deny that you had your way with that sweet, innocent, God-fearin', little gal of mine?"

Longarm took two quick steps and whacked Jesse Burton in the middle of the forehead with his pistol barrel. The flabbergasted saloon owner's eyes almost crossed out of their sockets. He hit the barber shop floor like a hundred-pound sack of chicken feed, dropped from a loading dock six feet above a farmer's waiting wagon bed.

Potter Burton's only son still quivered when Longarm called out, "You fellers come on back and drag this revolting stack of hammered horse dung out of my sight. He's stinkin' up Mr. Smoot's place of business and further irritating the hell out of me by just being here."

As the clearly shaken Tubbs brothers gathered up their boss and started toward the street for the second time, Eli stumbled under the limp, hard-to-manage load, then glared at Longarm. "You ain't heard the last of this, or of us, Marshal. You shoulda gone on ahead and kilt ole Jesse when you had the chance. He's a real hard case when it comes to 'at 'ere little gal of his 'n."

Longarm holstered his pistol. "Well, when he wakes up, you tell him to stay the hell away from me, Tubbs. I've listened to just about all the hot-mouthed horseshit I want to hear from the runtified squirt about Marley Newman. Near as I've been able to determine, the girl does pretty much as she pleases."

The smarter of the Tubbs brothers stumbled over the threshold, carrying his end of Jesse Burton's sagging body, and said, "Well, I can by God gar-damn-tee it won't do one bit of good, but I'll tell 'im what you went and said anyways."

Longarm followed his tormentors to the door, stood on the threshold and watched until they made their way down the street. By the time the trio reached the Onion's boardwalk, Jesse Burton appeared to have somewhat revived and managed to wobble back onto his feet. He stumbled through the saloon's doors supported and held up between the Tubbs brothers.

"He's right, Marshal."

Longarm turned and saw Josh Smoot holding a shotgun and standing in the back corner of the shop. "Reckon you would have used that big popper there, Josh?"

"Oh, I've no problem killing any man who's threatening me or mine. I could snuff out bastards like the Tubbs brothers and not miss a wink of sleep. They've bullied, beaten, stomped, and generally terrorized damned near everyone in town. Guess they'll probably plan on favoring me with a return visit, and more detailed attention, after the way this dance turned out."

Longarm snatched his snuff-colored Stetson off Josh Smoot's hat rack and carefully snugged it down on his head. "If the stupid sons of bitches give you any trouble at all while I'm still in town, you let me know. I'll see it doesn't happen again."

"Mighty kind of you, but you'd best look out for yourself, Marshal. Jesse Burton isn't above shooting you in the back from ambush, or having one of those idiot Tubbs brothers do it for him. The boy's nefarious. Ain't hardly a soul in town that hasn't had a potentially deadly run-in with him, at one time or another."

Smoot propped the heavy shotgun against the barbershop's wall, just inside the door, and followed Longarm out onto the boardwalk. Longarm leaned against a porch pillar and lit a nickel cheroot. Both men watched, with considerable interest, as three hard-looking riders, all squint-eyed and loaded down with iron, entered from the north end of town, rode slowly past the jail, and then made a beeline for Jesse Burton's saloon.

Covered in a fine layer of West Texas grime, the men appeared to have come from some distance. Their run-out, lathered horses drooped from the oppressive heat and the brutal exertion they had obviously expended. The gunmen's filthy yellow dusters whipped around on a hot wind that blew across Main Street. The heat, combined with the sullen parade of haggard dealers in death, caused those watching from the boardwalk that morning to break out in an instant sweat.

The gunny closest to Longarm, as the trio rode by, was minus a leg. He sported a carved wooden substitute that rested in a special leather stirrup which allowed him to ride with the nub stretched almost straight out like he was seated in a chair.

"This don't look real good," Smoot said out of the corner of his mouth. "This don't look good, a'tall, Marshal Long."

"You've put the saddle on the right horse with that observation, Josh. Can't see anything good coming out of this bunch."

"Do you know 'em, Marshal? Do you know those men?" Smoot asked under his breath, as though afraid the riders might hear.

Longarm shook his head, then blew cigar smoke skyward. A pronounced tinge of resignation had crept into his voice when he said, "Not really, Josh, but I'm pretty sure I know who they are."

"Who do you think they are?" Smoot sounded more than a bit concerned.

"If guessing means anything at all, they're probably Shooter, Stump, and Axel Moon—Hangtown Harry's three remaining murderous brothers. Real easy to spot ole Stump. Killers, every one of them. Not the kind of men to turn your back on."

"Damnation."

"Damn right. Ain't no doubt about it, Josh. It's just like my ole white-haired granddaddy use to say. When it rains, it does tend to pour, even in bone dry West Texas weather like this. Well, guess maybe I should have snatched ole Harry up, and dragged his more than sorry ass out of that cell the minute I got here and headed back to Fort Stockton as fast as we could ride. Probably already be there by now and on my way back to Denver."

Smoot shook his head. "Well, I don't know 'bout that, Marshal. 'Course I'm a rank amateur, when it comes to the man-huntin' and outlaw-transportin' business, and such. But, seems to me, it would prove a lot worse decision to get caught out in the big cold and lonely by a bunch

122

of armed killers like them as just rode down the street. Be better all the way around, if you should have to confront 'em, to do it here in Panther Mountain. Wouldn't it?"

"I suppose you're right." Steeped in thought, Longarm rolled the cheroot around between his fingers for several seconds. Then he said, "Wonder if you'd do me a favor, Josh?"

"I'm willing to help you any way I can, Marshal Long. All you have to do is name it."

"Well, don't go jumping in the pit before you count all the snakes and understand exactly how many I expect you to stomp for me."

"I'm certain that whatever you have in mind won't be easy, but I'm willing and able to do whatever I can."

"Look, Josh, Buster took off yesterday. Said he wanted to see his family. While that might have been the God's truth, the man hasn't bothered to come back yet, or let me know what the hell he's doing. I need to pay a visit on an old friend of my boss's today. Don't plan on being gone long, but do have to leave for a spell. And, as you can see, because of Buster's continued absence, the jail's totally unattended when I have to be out."

"I understand. You want me to watch over the place for you while you're gone?"

"Actually, think I require a bit more than just watching over the place. Situation would be better, all the way around, if you could take that big double-barreled popper of yours, lock and bar the jailhouse door, and sit over there at Buster's desk till I can get back. Reckon you could do that for me?"

Smoot scratched a smooth, closely-shaved chin, then ran trembling fingers through his thinning hair. "Don't see why I couldn't sit in for a spell. Not much for me to do around here today. Hadn't been for your shave, I doubt

I'd have made another dime, as slow as business has been lately. Sure, Marshal Long, I can do that for you."

"Your cooperation might prove dangerous, Josh. You understand that, don't you?"

"Oh, yes, understand completely."

"Good. I'll get you some help if I can. One more man sure as hell wouldn't hurt anything. Tell you what, give me a few minutes. Then, come on over. Once I'm gone, want you, and whoever else I can get to lend a hand, to padlock, and double-bar the front door." Longarm turned, laid his hand on Smoot's shoulder, and welded the man to the spot with a stern gaze. "If anyone should try to get inside the jail that shouldn't be in there, like either or all of the three we just saw pass, and anyone other than Buster Byers, I don't want you to hesitate for a second. Blast the hell out of them. You understand my feelings on this, Josh?"

"Oh, absolutely, Marshal Long. You've got my word. I'll do exactly as you asked. No one will get inside the jail while I'm on guard for you. I promise."

"I'll have to be gone for two, or maybe three, hours. My absence shouldn't be a problem. It's always been my experience, in the past, that no matter how important the mission, soft-headed goobers like the Moon brothers are more focused on getting good and juiced up after a long, hot ride than anything else they might have in mind."

"Whiskey brave, huh?"

"Yep. That's the way I see it. Rumors I've heard in the past would indicate the entire family wasn't born, but rudely squeezed out of a bartender's rag. If that's anything close to the truth, the whole bunch has to get good and liquored up before they can generate enough nerve to act. That should give me a bit of time to get ready for them."

124

"You think this situation's going to end up with clouds of hot lead in the air, no matter how you cut it?"

Longarm stepped off the boardwalk and started ambling back to the jail. Over his shoulder he said, "Not going to lie to you. I don't own any crystal balls. Can't be sure about what's about to happen either way, Josh. But whether we like it or not, we're going to find out exactly what the Moon boys have in mind pretty soon."

Chapter 15

Jesus Sanchez and the beast, Diablo, were waiting when Longarm climbed the porch treads to Panther Mountain's jail. He stopped beside the boy, gazed back up the street, and watched, narrow-eyed, as the Moon brothers climbed off their haggered mounts in the midst of a thick cloud of swirling grit. The men tied the weary animals to a hitch rail in front of the Red Onion, slapped at the grime on their filthy dusters, and then bulled their way across the boardwalk, and disappeared through the cow-country oasis's swinging doors.

As though preoccupied, Longarm mumbled, "Got all your chores done, Jesus?"

"*Sí, señor, mi trabajo es completo.*"

"That's mighty good. Mighty good. Now then, want you to pay close attention. I have an important question I need to ask."

"*Sí*, I understand, Señor Long. An important question to ask. Of course, I will try my best to answer."

"That's fine. Mighty fine. Now listen, son, do you by any chance know where a gent named Mica Hatchett hangs his hat?"

A mystified look blanketed the boy's face when he glanced up at Longarm. "Hangs his hat, señor? Hangs his hat? I do not understand. I do not know these things."

Longarm came back to himself and sharpened his inquiry. "Ah. Well, what I meant was where he lives? Do you know where he lives? It's very important I find him."

As the boy stroked the sitting Diablo's enormous, panting head, his ebony eyes widened to the point where Longarm could see the whites all the way around them. "You are the *amigo grande* of the famous gunfighter Mica Hatchett, Señor Long? *Es muy bien.*"

Somewhat surprised by the boy's obvious admiration for, or perhaps fear of, Mica Hatchett, Longarm said, "No, can't say as how I know the man at all. Not really. His was a name my superiors gave me in case I should find myself in need of someone's help. You appear to have some knowledge of where he can be found."

"Oh, *sí*. Everyone in Panther Mountain knows where his excellency, Señor Hatchett, lives. Even the smallest of children know of, and fear, the man."

"How long would it take us to get to his place from here?"

The boy stood and pointed back over his shoulder to the west. "It is not far—a ride of perhaps five miles to the mountain, then another half-mile up. Ours is not so great a mountain, señor. Even so, getting to the peak is a treacherous and difficult trip, once you reach the trail that snakes its way to the top. But you must be aware, Marshal, I do not think Señor Hatchett likes to be disturbed. No, I do not think he likes being bothered by visitors at all."

Longarm placed a comforting hand on the boy's skinny shoulder. "Can't say as how I blame him much for such feelings, Jesus, but I need to talk with the man, and mighty quick. Marshal Byers hasn't made it back yet and, to be absolutely truthful, I'm beginning to think he just might not come back."

"Es verdad, señor?"

"I'd be willing to bet that if the news about Moon's murderous family arriving in town gets to ole Buster, we'll likely never see the man again. Given that possibility, I just might require Mica Hatchett's help real soon."

Jesus cast a knowing glance toward the Red Onion Saloon and said, "I saw those men when they rode in—those bad men. They carried many guns, Marshal. They all looked very much like Señor Moon. Perhaps *hermanos*, his brothers, no?"

"Bad men, yes. Armed to the teeth, you bet. Brothers, probably. Willing to kill everyone in town to get Hangtown Harry loose, wouldn't surprise me in the least."

"And you believe Señor Hatchett can help you with these terrible men?"

"Well, I certainly hope so. Now, here's what we're going to do. In a few minutes, Mr. Smoot will be coming over. He's agreed to look after the jail while we're gone. You get the key. Show him how to lock everything up. Once he arrives, I'll head over to Newman's. Gonna pick up my horse and get you something to ride as well."

Jesus Sanchez's face glowed with the pride of newfound responsibility. "Oh, yes, Señor Long. I understand. I will see to everything. You need not concern yourself any further. I will take care of Señor Smoot. Do you have any special message I should give him when he arrives?"

"Let me think a second." Longarm scratched his chin and gazed back down the street. "Tell you what, Jesus, you needn't worry about Smoot just yet. We've already talked anyway. He knows exactly what to expect. Leastways, I hope he does. Right now I've got a special errand I want you to run."

Excited at the prospect of immediate action, Jesus flashed a huge grin, snatched his hole-riddled, palm-leaf hat off and said, "*Sí*, Señor Long, I am ready. What must I do?"

"Want you to hoof it down to the Wagon Wheel and fetch Braxton Pike here for me."

"The *pistolero*, señor?"

"Yes, the *pistolero*. Bring him back here as quickly as possible. Don't dawdle. I need to speak to him immediately. Do whatever you have to do, but make the man understand the urgency of my request, Jesus. Do it now." The boy nodded, and disappeared in a churning swirl of bare feet and flying dust with the dog in hot pursuit.

Shotgun in hand, Josh Smoot arrived at the jail only a few seconds ahead of Jesus and Braxton Pike. Longarm immediately detected Smoot's unease with the gunman's threatening presence and quickly moved to allay any of his good friend's fears.

"Glad you could come with so little notice, Brax. I do appreciate your speedy response."

In a gesture of bold confidence, Pike placed the palms of his hands against his pistol's butts and pushed them forward. "Told you I'd help if you asked, Marshal. From what I just saw ride down the street a few minutes ago, looks to me like you're gonna need more'n a little assistance once them Moon boys get finished tankin' up on liquid bravery."

"You know, Josh Smoot, Brax?" Longarm asked as he waved the men toward each other.

Pike held out his hand, and they shook. "'Course we know each other. Josh been shaving me two, maybe three times a week ever since I got to town."

Longarm nodded. "Good. Now here's what I want the two of you to do. I've got to make a quick trip up on Pan-

130

ther Mountain. Want you boys to stay here. Keep an eye on the jail. Jesus and I shouldn't be gone any more than two, maybe three hours."

Pike strutted around Buster Byers's desk and flopped into the absent marshal's squeaky chair. He pushed his hat to the back of his head with one finger and said, "Hell, that's easy enough."

"I've already told Josh what I expect," Longarm said as he snatched up his Winchester. "Don't let anyone in until I get back. That plain enough, Brax."

"*Absolutamente, mi amigo.* As long as I'm here, ain't no one coming in this jail. 'Specially them Moon boys down at the Onion." He pulled a pistol, flipped the loading gate open, and rolled the cylinder. "But I have to admit, Long, sure do wish they'd try. Give me a damned good reason, and excellent opportunity, to kill a couple of 'em."

Longarm pulled the door open and motioned Jesus outside. "Don't do any shooting unless it simply can't be avoided. But if you're forced, don't hesitate. Now, lock and bar the door when I close it. I'll be back in three hours."

Chapter 16

In the beginning, it appeared to Longarm that the ride out to the foothills of Panther Mountain was something of an adventure for Jesus and his monstrous companion. As they waded across Panther Creek, the boy's obvious pleasure at having his own animal to ride, seeming knowledge of where they were headed, and delight at being the center of attention, entertained and pleased him to no end.

Longarm watched with some amusement as the boy and the dog frolicked in the creek and enjoyed themselves immensely. But they rode on and eventually came off the flat, arid plain between the town and the imposing, almost mile-high peak of Panther Mountain itself. As the tiny band made its way into the peak's low, ragged foothills, Jesus quickly lost much of the initial delight that had colored his actions when the ride began. The boy's laughter and smiles quickly vanished. He became nervous, quieter, and much more cautious.

The peckerwood-sized posse halted at the mountain's sparse, sun-blistered tree line. Jesus searched back and forth for the trail he said would take them directly to Mica Hatchett's remote and hard-to-access home. After a bit of determined effort, and a degree of edgy exertion, the boy and dog finally found a barely detectable pathway that resembled the kind of trail used by wild pigs. The coarse, almost invisible, route snaked its way upward between large, sharp-edged boulders.

As Longarm followed his now almost silent guide and rounded the first huge rock, Jesus apprehensively pointed to one side. Hanging from a bark-covered post, a coarsely-made sign emblazoned with a burned-in message read: KEEP OFF. THIS IS HATCHETT'S ROAD. GO BACK NOW.

Longarm barely heard Jesus when he said, "You see, Marshal. Señor Hatchett does not care for visitors."

"Would seem so, but our visit today can't be helped."

"Not many people come here," the boy called over his skinny shoulder, in a voice not much louder than a coarse whisper.

"Can you read that sign, Jesus?" Longarm asked.

"No, but I've been told many times what it says by those who can. In town that sign, and all the others along the way, is *muy famoso*."

"There are others, huh? Well, don't worry yourself, son. I sincerely doubt Mica Hatchett would do anything terrible to a child."

"Everyone knows that you are not to travel on Señor Hatchett's road. All my life, I have heard many strange stories told of those *la gente* who violated the warning and were never seen again."

Longarm chuckled at the brutality of the myth and said, "Did you, by chance, know any of the people who disappeared, never to be seen again? Haven't lost any family members, brothers, sisters, or maybe cousins, up here on this trail, have you?"

"Oh, no, señor but I am certain there have been dozens who have never come back. The entire town knows that

Señor Hatchett is a dangerous and violent man. Feared by all who've met him. *Sí*, everyone knows this."

"Does Hatchett ever come into town?"

"Very seldom. There are those who claim that to look upon Señor Hatchett is to look upon the face of your own death. I, myself, have gazed upon him only once. And that was from the shelter and safety of my hidden spot under the jail's front porch."

"You hid when he rode past?"

"*Sí*. I hid there, and even got down behind Diablo, so as not to be noticed. I watched the man ride past on his tall white horse. But my fear was great. I was too frightened. Could not dare to look upon his face. He carried his famous gun that day."

"Famous gun? What famous gun are you talking about?"

"The gun he wrenched from the hands of Death himself, señor. Pale as the bleached bones of the long dead and gleaming of the Devil's gold. The gun that has had all the life sucked out of it by *Satanás*'s red-eyed demons from the fiery pit. You will see. Most likely just before he kills us with it. You will see, Marshal."

"Well, you mustn't be afraid. Trust me. I can assure you there's no reason to fear Mica Hatchett."

A tremor in Jesus's voice belied a childish bravado when he said, "It is well you are here, señor. So long as I ride by your side, I have no fear of Señor Hatchett."

The narrow, crooked, rock-littered trace climbed ever upward. Demanding, and dangerous in places, the path zigzagged back and forth between steep walls of wind and sand-weathered stone. In some spots, their horses had difficulty passing through the restricted openings allowed them. The animal's hooves clattered and skated across sloped, slatelike shelves of stone and, at one espe-

135

cially confining point, the available gap proved so limited that Longarm and the boy found it necessary to dismount and lead their animals through.

The lawman's usually rock-steady nerves began to fray and got little relief as they slowly proceeded from one obstacle to the next. At various intervals, all along the torturous way, additional signs, each with a more graphic message than the last, warned of dire consequences to anyone who stupidly ventured upon Hatchett's constricted, agonizing road. Longarm began to wonder if his bold predictions for Jesus's safety just might prove misplaced.

After what seemed like an hour of negotiating the labyrinthine maze under a sun that bored through a man's hat like a white-hot auger, the pathway abruptly opened onto a broad, breathtakingly beautiful, lush plateau. The sweeping and amazingly green spot appeared to encircle most of the entire east side of the mountain's gently sloping face.

Against Panther Mountain's upward slant, and seemingly built directly into the rock, sat a rambling, board and batten cabin built of hard-weathered lumber. The few observable windows were covered with stretched animal skins, but opened to the sweet-smelling air. Vegetable and flower gardens sprouted randomly around the entire verdant plot. And, most impressive of all, the cabin wall that faced the road was covered with a lattice work burdened down with the largest, blood-red roses Longarm had ever seen.

Several horses, including a long-legged solid white gelding, eyed their visitors from inside a rail corral on the far side of the rose-covered dwelling. A clear stream bubbling directly from between massive stones along the farthest edge of a primitive lean-to shelter provided for the horses and continued across the flat grass-covered terrain, then darted down the mountain's face toward Panther Creek and the town.

Longarm and Jesus reined up a few steps from the cabin's battered front porch. A pair of scruffy ladder-backed, cane-bottomed chairs worn fuzzy by use, sat on either side of the only visible door. Two saddles under repair, a variety of tools and tack mending equipment, a pile of used and rusted horseshoes, and near half a dozen diamond-backed rattlesnake skins stretched over flat planks, covering almost every square inch of available space on the cramped and littered veranda.

Longarm called out, "Hello the house. Are you there, Mr. Hatchett?"

Jesus looked uneasy and squirmed in the saddle on his rented paint pony. He jumped and trembled when Longarm again shouted, "Mr. Hatchett, name's Custis Long. I'm a deputy United States marshal. I need to speak with you, sir. Is anyone at home?"

The single plank door creaked open on leather hinges. A tall, raw-boned man stepped through the narrow opening. Mica Hatchett was dressed in the rough clothing typical of a working ranch hand. His weather-beaten, white-bearded face was highlighted by a full head of shoulder-length hair of the same color. A wide, rattlesnake belt over a fringed, leather shirt encircled a narrow waist, and a leather string decorated with a number of massive animal teeth dangled from his long, thin, sun-bronzed neck.

Taken altogether, Billy Vail's old *amigo* sported the stunning appearance most Bible-thumping, churchgoers would have, without hesitation, described as the image held in their hearts of how God probably looked on a good day.

In addition to his startling appearance, the strange-looking vision carried the most remarkable weapon Longarm had ever seen. The short, double-barreled shot-gun's stock and forearm looked to have been shaped from a single chunk of ivory, and both were heavily embellished with fancy carvings. The entire length of the barrel, the receiver, hammers, even the trigger and guard, were washed in gold. The gun glittered fiercely in spite of being shaded from the bright sunshine by a sloped, wood-shingled roof over the cabin's cluttered porch.

When he finally spoke, Hatchett even sounded like a deity—an angry Lord God Almighty about to hand down a new set of commandments from atop some Biblical mountain. "Last time I bothered to count, there's sixteen signs along the path warning idiots like you to keep off my road and away from my home," he growled.

"You're absolutely right, sir. We saw them all. Read each and every one," Longarm replied.

Hatchett shook his head as though unbelieving. "Then what exactly about the words *keep off my road*, *stay away*, or *go back now*, don't you understand, Deputy United States Marshal Long? Were you born stupid? Did you, by chance, grow up that way? Are you simple-minded? Or was the veil of unparalleled foolishness simply thrust upon you as time passed, and you kept getting older and dumber? The reason I ask is because even the most ill-informed peon from hereabouts heeds the messages on my signs."

Longarm nodded, and smiled under the weight of Hatchett's adroit verbal attack. Then, his head snapped up and he stared the older man directly in the eye. "Mr. Hatchett, my immediate superior, Marshal Billy Vail of Denver, said if I ever needed help while visiting in Panther Mountain, Texas, I should make it a point to seek out his old friend Mica."

Hatchett's distant, surly, almost arrogant demeanor appeared to change immediately with the mention of the U.S. marshal's handle. An expression of surprise and unexpected pleasure spread across the old ranger's rugged face. "You mean to tell me that you know Billy Vail?"

"I do indeed, sir. I've worked for Billy a number of years now. Spoke with him less than a week ago. He serves as the United States marshal for the federal district court in Denver."

The white-haired man shook his head. He blinked as though befuddled by the news of an old and long forgotten friend who had somehow appeared like a ghost from behind a magic curtain. Then, he eased the hammers down on his strange and magnificent scattergun. "United States marshal, huh? You know, Long, I haven't seen ole Billy in years. So many years in fact, I can't even call to mind the last time we talked. Didn't realize he'd managed to work himself up to such lofty heights. United States marshal, for real and true, huh? Now that's a caution, if ever there was one. Must admit I never expected a man of such grossly limited intelligence to go so far in this world."

Longarm chuckled, crossed his arms, and leaned forward on the McClellan saddle's abbreviated horn. "Truly amazing stuff when a man bothers to think on it for very long. Does tend to demonstrate the power of politics, don't it? Anyhow, he said the two of you became friends while working as Texas Rangers, and implied, that if properly asked, you'd likely tell me the tale of how your friendship came about. It's a story I'd enjoy hearing someday, when you have the time, and the inclination, of course."

"Really warn't much to it. Just a whole lot of blood, thunder, and Comanche killin'. Kind of stuff you've probably already seen more'n your own share of by now. Must admit, though, some parts of the experiences we shared did have their high points."

"I would consider it a privilege to hear you tell the tale someday—especially those high points."

Hatchett made a half-hearted motion in the direction of Jesus and the dog. "Who're your friends?"

Longarm relaxed, smiled, and nodded in the boy's direction. "These are my posse men, Mr. Hatchett. Jesus takes care of Marshal Buster Byers's jail down in town. In spite of being very much afraid of you, he bravely led me here today. Weren't for Jesus I might not have found this place."

"And the dog's name? That damned thing is a dog, ain't it?"

"Jesus calls his hairy friend there, Diablo. Best advice I can give you about the shaggy, Mexican devil is that if it was me, I wouldn't mess with him, unless somehow possessed with an overpowering urge to lose a hand, or perhaps even an entire arm."

Hatchett lowered the shotgun and leaned it against the inside of the cabin's door frame. "Well, I suppose now that you're both here, might as well step on down and set a spell. You can give your animals a rest, and tell me how I might be able to help you out. Not sure exactly what, if anything, I can do, but I'm always willing to listen."

As Longarm climbed off his animal, Hatchett added, "Take one of the chairs, Marshal. It's a bit cooler out here on the porch than it is inside. Just cooked some coffee, if'n you'd care for a cup. Was about to take one my ownself and have a sit down out here to contemplate God's splendor, for a spell."

"Coffee sounds mighty good, Mica. Think a cup would really hit the spot right now."

While Hatchett went for the coffee, Longarm gathered the reins of Jesus's pony, then led both animals to the rail corral. He turned them loose inside the enclosure to roam about at will.

By the time Longarm had finished with the horses, Hatchett had returned carrying battered tin cups of steaming, fresh-brewed belly wash for all three of them. Jesus sat on the porch steps, sipped from his cup and beamed with the pride of being included.

Fully aware that every man has his favorite chair, Longarm waited until his host had selected the one on the porch he preferred before sitting himself.

Hatchett stretched his long, thin legs out and, after a minute of uninterrupted quiet had passed, he said, "Might as well get right down to it, Marshal Long. What can I do for you?"

Longarm leaned forward, elbows on knees, and gazed unflinchingly into Hatchett's ice-blue eyes. "Mica, I came down here to pick up a killer named Hangtown Harry Moon. Marshal Byers threw him into the Panther Mountain jail about two weeks ago and then informed the United States marshal of his capture. There's a sizable outstanding reward on the man for the murder of a federal judge, and Buster has his eyes on it. Unfortunately, I made the mistake of staying over a bit longer than I probably should have. Now, Moon's brothers have arrived on the scene. I have absolutely no doubt they'll likely try their deadly best to set him free."

Hatchett stared into his cup. "Haven't done anything so far, have they?"

"Nothing. Evil bunch just rode in this very morning.

There's three of them, and that's not even close to the ugly whole of it."

"What else then?"

"Had a run-in with the owner of the Red Onion Saloon—belligerent little shit named Jesse Burton. As a consequence, I not only have to worry about Hangtown Harry Moon's idiot family, but Jesse Burton and his henchmen as well."

The ice-blue eyes drilled Longarm to his chair as Hatchett said, "Well, damn, son. Have you made any other enemies I need to know about since you arrived?"

Longarm shook his head. "Not completely sure, to tell the honest truth. Killed a drunken gunman who was running with the Moon clan and tried to get Hangtown Harry loose. He was out to inflate his reputation and just wasn't up to beating a shotgun. His name was Willy Coffin. That happened not long after I got here. Have a pair of his friends locked up in the Panther Mountain jail, right this very minute. And I've had words with a gun slick who works down at the Wagon Wheel—feller name of Braxton Pike. By the time that conversation ended, he offered to help me with Moon, should I need it. So, I took him up on his offer."

"My God, been busy since you got to town, ain't you, son? Take it from what I just heard, you don't trust Braxton Pike all that much."

"No. Not entirely. Don't really have any good reason not to, other than my knowledge of the man's past reputation. Hell, he was civil enough when we talked. Never hesitated when I asked him to help with the jail while I was up here. Problem is, I could very well be forced to bring him in on more of this deal than I'd planned on before the whole dance has a chance to completely play out."

"What about Buster Byers?"

"Well, now there's a damned good question and another reason why I'm here right now. Just can't be sure how far I can trust ole Buster, either. Don't think he'd go so far as to be party to any harm that might befall me, because that would delay payment of his reward for Hangtown Harry. But I have serious doubts he'd stick around to help if Moon's family decided to kill me and break their brother out of his jail."

The steaming cup came away from Hatchett's lips. He blew across the hot liquid's surface, then said, "Sounds like you've gone and wedged yerself between the proverbial rock and hard place, Marshal Long. Seems to me that gettin' Hangtown Harry back to Denver might end up bein' a site harder'n scratchin' a porcupine's belly."

Longarm leaned over with his elbows on his knees and stared at his feet. "Yep. Before it all shakes out, the whole damnable mess could turn into a blood-saturated head scratcher for sure."

Hatchett pushed his chair up on its hind legs and leaned it against the cabin wall. "If ye're here and Buster's off somewhere else, who's watching the jail and your prisoners?"

"Pike and a feller named Smoot."

"The undertaker?"

"Yeah. Nice man. He buried Willy Coffin for me."

"Josh Smoot is about as fine a gent as ye're likely to come across in this part of the country. But I've never known him as anything fancy with a gun."

"Well, he's supposed to be sitting at Buster Byers's desk right now, holding a long-barreled scattergun pointed at the front door. Told him I wouldn't be gone any longer than necessary—two hours, maybe three."

"Sounds to me like we need to dump the rest of this coffee out. Head back to town as quick as we can, Marshal Long. God only knows what might have occurred in the short time you've been out of pocket."

Longarm took one last pull at his cup, then said, "I think you're right, Mica. Sooner the better. But first, think I'd best make everything official. Make you a deputy."

Hatchett smiled. "Been a long while since I actually got made legitimate for something like this, Marshal Long."

"Well, sure there's those who wouldn't even bother, but I believe in doing things the right way. Have absolutely no doubt we just might have to kill some bad people shortly. Best see to the legalities. Hold up your right hand."

Hatchett did as told, and, in short order, Longarm exercised his power to deputize by administering a brief oath designed to take care of any questions that might arise should lethal force be necessary in seeing to it that Hangtown Harry Moon got back to Denver alive, kicking and in suitable shape for a hanging.

Chapter 17

Jesus and Diablo led the way down the narrow, twisted trail to Mica Hatchett's Panther Mountain home, across the shallow, slow-moving creek, and, eventually, along the dusty road that led back into town.

As the party reined in their tired mounts in front of Newman's Livery, Longarm glanced along the length of the main thoroughfare. Doors and windows on the remaining active businesses, normally open, appeared closed or shuttered. Harlan's Grocery and both saloons looked like the only establishments ready and waiting for commerce.

Longarm lifted and resettled his pistol belt. "Mighty quiet, don't you think, Mica? Not a solitary soul on the street." He stepped down from the bay's brawny back and slapped the reins against a sweaty palm. "You can usually hear piano music from the saloons. Not today. Nothing. Way too quiet to suit me."

Hatchett climbed off his mount, then slipped the glistening, golden shotgun from its leather bindings. He breeched the weapon, checked the loads, and snapped it shut with a resounding click. Then, he pulled a cartridge belt solid with brass shotgun shells, off his saddle horn. He threw the belt over his shoulder, gazed in the direction of the Red Onion, then said, "Yeah, and there's half a dozen animals I've never seen before tied down yonder at the Onion's hitch rack. Just the kind of thing that could make a suspicious man wonder if something might be afoot, don't you think?"

Walker Newman poked his weary head from between the barely cracked, sun and wind-weathered doors of the livery, then scurried over like a scared rabbit to take charge of their animals. "Glad to see you back, Marshal Long," he said. "Been some more rough lookin' fellers hit town over the past few hours. As you can surely see, they've went and scared the bejabbers out of most folks. Everyone's done scurried for their favorite hidey hole like a bunch of scared rabbits. 'Cept maybe ole man Harlan. Son of a bitch loves money a damned site more'n livin'."

Longarm waved in the general direction of the Wagon Wheel and the Red Onion. "Haven't harmed anyone, done anything wayward yet, have they?"

Newman ran a quaking hand under his sweat-drenched hat and scratched his head. "Not as I know of. Nope. Not as I know of. It's just that three more of 'em showed up 'bout an hour after you and Jesus rode out this mornin'. Mean lookin' trio, too. Damned lot of iron strapped on 'em. 'Bout as bad a bunch as I ever seen. That's includin' them three as came in a-fore. 'Tween 'em they sure as shootin' cleared out the Onion. Ain't no one down there now 'cept these new fellers. At least six of 'em now, near as I can tell, Marshal. 'Course, guess I done forgot 'bout Jesse and the Tubbs brothers. Hell, that makes nine or ten, give or take one or two, here and there."

Hatchett propped the golden shotgun on one shoulder. "Sounds, for damned sure, like Hangtown Harry's clan is gatherin' up enough firepower to bust him loose." He shot Longarm a stern glance. "We'd best be hoofin' on over to the jail and gettin' ourselves ready for whatever Moon's friends, and loony, murderous family, have got in mind."

Longarm turned, stared up at the still mounted Jesus, then placed his hand on the boy's knee. "Need you to go find Marshal Byers, *mi amigo*. Tell him to get back up here to the jail, as soon as possible. Explain everything you've seen and heard. Be quick, *amigo*."

"*Si*, señor. Jesus will do as you ask." He kicked the paint pony's sides. Longarm slapped its rump, and the boy started for the south end of town at a gallop. Diablo trailed behind.

"*Rápido, amigo, rápido*," Longarm called through the thick cloud of floating grime the boy left behind. Then, he turned to Hatchett and said, "You're right. Might as well stroll on over to the jail. Imagine Josh and Brax are ready for some relief."

As Longarm and Hatchett trudged toward Panther Mountain's stronghold of a jail, he spotted several men he'd not seen before. They filed out of the Onion's front door, pointed, and eyeballed Jesus as the boy sped past. Longarm kept a close watch on the strangers and called out to the men inside Panther Mountain's lockup, before he stepped onto the raised boardwalk in front of Marshal Buster Byers's office. Joshua Smoot threw the jailhouse door open with a flourish.

"Jesus, Josh, you look like a man who's just been saved from drowning in muddy water," Longarm said.

"Please come in. Come inside quick, Marshal. Get yourselves off the street," Smoot said and waved them off the porch. "My God, I'm glad you're back," the undertaker almost shouted as he clapped Longarm on the back. "We've had another group of gunnies hit town since you left." He pointed a trembling finger in the Red Onion's direction. "Must be half a dozen of 'em down at the Onion, right this very minute, not to mention your friends Jesse Burton and the Tubbs boys."

Longarm ambled over to Buster Byers's desk and laid his Henry rifle down in front of Braxton Pike. Pike locked him in a steely gaze and said, "Pot's a bubblin', Marshal. Killers are a gatherin' like a pack of hungry wolves. Like Mr. Smoot said, we've had at least three more of 'em come in while you were gone. Situation here ain't lookin' good a'tall."

"I know. Just spoke with Walker Newman over at the livery. He told me all about it. Think I just now saw those same fellers come out on the boardwalk as Jesus rode by on his way to fetch Buster."

Pike let bootless feet, covered in hole-riddled socks, drop from the desktop to the floor. He sat straight up in the complaining chair, bent over at the waist, and began pulling at one of his boots. "Bet you everything I've got on me you'll never see Buster again."

Longarm snatched his hat off and dropped it on the desk beside the rifle. "You sound mighty certain about that."

"Have reason to be fairly certain. See, I recognized one of 'em fellers. Dangerous man, Long. 'Bout as dangerous as you could ever imagine. Actually surprised me some to see him. And if I know Buster, he's already heard the news and won't be seen anywhere near this jail till the coming storm blows over." He stamped his foot to get it settled in the boot, then pawed around under the chair until he found the mate.

Hatchett dragged a ladder-backed chair up to a spot at

one end of the desk, twirled it around, and sat. He laid the shotgun across his lap, leaned his arms across the top rail of the chair and said, "Well, get on with it, Brax. Go ahead and give us the bad news. Who'd you see?"

Pike glanced up at Hatchett from his socked foot and grinned. Hatchett glared back and made a gimme motion with one hand. "Stop doin' your cat-ate-the-canary act, Brax. Who'd you see?"

"The one and only Clyde Stillwell," the gunman said.

Joshua Smoot gasped out loud at mention of the name, twirled around like a crazed ballet dancer, and pulled at his hair. Hatchett shook his head and stared at the floor.

Red-faced and trembling, Smoot squeaked, "Jesus, you didn't bother to inform me of that. Why didn't you bother to tell me you recognized a murderous beast like Clyde Stillwell, Brax?"

Longarm shook his head, rubbed one temple, then said, "Who the hell's Clyde Stillwell?"

Hatchett pulled his hat off and dropped it over one knee. "He's a south Texas killer for hire. Don't usually even show his face, unless they's murder to be done and money to be made. 'Course, he's managed to get away with murderin' the hell out of folks for years. Somebody shoulda hung the son of a bitch a long time ago. Rumor has it, he's a bosom *compadre* of shooter Moon's. Story most folks like to pass around is all about how they met during a jail stay down in Del Rio, some years back."

"Well, if he's here, he's here, and there's nothing we can do about it now. Any attempts been made to get inside the jail during my absence?" Longarm asked.

Josh Smoot stopped pulling his hair and pacing the floor long enough to say, "No. Only person we've seen is Armondo. Mex from next door. He brought food for the prisoners twice while you were out. Have to admit ole

Buster does feed these bastards pretty well, in spite of all their complaining."

Longarm pulled a cheroot from his vest pocket, held the stogie between his fingers and pointed at the huge door to the cell block. "What about our prisoners, Brax. Had any trouble with any of them?"

"Nope. Fact is, now that you mention it, we ain't heard one sound out of 'em ever since you left for Mica's place. Not a peep. All three of 'em been quiter'n church mice. You'd think they actually knew something was about to happen, if'n you ask me."

Longarm shoved the cheroot into his mouth and scratched a Lucifer to life beneath it. He puffed on the smoke, flicked a sprig of tobacco off his tongue, then said, "If this same situation fell to you, Brax, and by some odd, offhand chance you found yourself in the company of Moon's friends and family, how do you think they would handle what they've discovered since arriving in Panther Mountain?"

Pike leaned back in his chair, and clasped both hands behind his head. He gazed at the ceiling for several seconds, then said, "Not sure what I'd do, given that I wouldn't be caught dead in the company of any of the sorrier'n possum shit Moon family. But I can tell you, for certain sure, what the whole Moon bunch is doin' right at this exact very minute."

Longarm grinned and said, "Can't wait to hear it."

Pike had warmed up to the conversation and leaned forward, elbows on knees. "All six of 'em sons of bitches, the Moon boys and the other three, are down there at the Onion gettin' themselves good and drunk, so they can dredge up enough courage to come down here, reared up on their hind legs, call us out into the street, kill all of us, and take Hangtown Harry out of that cell back yonder."

Smoot clasped his head between his hands as though he'd been hit with a severe headache. "Sweet Merciful Father," he murmured.

Longarm turned to his stricken friend. "Just be calm, Josh. So far you've played virtually no part in this whole affair. I doubt any of the Moon boys will come looking specifically for you."

Smoot darted to the door, jerked it open, then stopped on the threshold with his hand on the knob. "I'm grateful for everything you did for me, Marshal Long. Truly, I do appreciate the opportunities you provided and the money I made from Willy Coffin's funeral. But I'm not a gunman, not by the wildest stretch of anyone's fevered imagination. You'll have to do without my active, gun-carrying assistance from here on in, whatever might occur." And with that he slammed the door shut and was gone.

Longarm strode to a window and watched his friend hustle back across the street to Smoot's Furniture, Undertaking, Funeral Parlor, Veterinary, Barber Shop and Bath House. He puffed on his fresh cheroot and said, "Kind of like the cowboy who got bit on the ass by a rattler; guess this is where we find out exactly who our real friends are."

Pike pushed the chair away and moved to a spot at the window beside Longarm. "Hell, you can't really blame the man much. You know as well as I do that the Moon clan'll kill us all, don't you? That is, unless we take the fight right to 'em."

Longarm flicked ashes from his smoke onto the floor. "Yeah, unfortunately, that's the way I've got it figured, too. Just no way in hell for them to break into a jail built like this one, unless maybe the Moon boys can get their hands on some explosives. Way I've got it figured, they've probably already realized that we can't stay locked behind these doors forever. Most likely, they'll try to pick us off one at a time while we're outside these walls for any reason I'm sure you can easily imagine— food, water, whatever. Suppose we could be stuck here for a spell."

Mica Hatchett stood, turned his chair around to face the other men, sat back down, and said, "No point just sittin' around here waitin' for them idiots to act. Why don't we just gut up, load up, and march down to the Onion and get this dance over and done with? What say you, boys? Wake up this mornin' with enough balls for a bit of black powder smoke, blood and thunder?"

Pike chuckled. "You're a man after my own heart, Hatchett. Known since the day I arrived in town I wouldn't want a man like you after my hide. So, if it comes to a vote, I say we stroll on down the street, kill as many of 'em snakes as possible. We go to dillydallin' around and it could get us all killed deader'n Julius Caesar."

The words had barely escaped Pike's lips when the office's front door burst open and ricocheted off the wall with a thunderous clap. Walker Newman stumbled inside like a blind man. Tears streamed down his soot and dust smudged cheeks. His lips moved but nothing came out for several seconds. Finally, in a barely audible voice, he managed to say, "Killed my beautiful daughter. The sorry son of a bitch done went and killed my Marley."

Longarm lept to the hostler's side, grabbed him by the arm, and ushered the stricken man to a rope-backed, cane-bottomed chair Hatchett had recently vacated. All three men gathered around Newman as he dropped into the seat like a man falling through the trap of a brand new gallows. His head appeared to bury itself between folded shoulders as though his entire upper body was somehow trying to cave in on itself.

With a shaking hand resting on the distraught man's

shoulder, Longarm's words trembled when he said, "What in the . . . blue-eyed hell . . . are you saying, Mr. Newman? Who killed your daughter? When? Where?"

Newman's empty-eyed gaze turned in the direction of the marshal's voice, but the poor man appeared not to see him or anything else in the room. He sounded as though speaking from the bottom of a rain barrel when he said, "Burton. Jesse Burton. He murdered my Marley. Done it right across the street in my own stable. Has to be him. Cain't be anyone else. Must've happened when I left, for just a few minutes, earlier today."

"How long ago?" Longarm asked.

"Not really certain. He came by, you see, and I left 'em alone. Comes by all the time like that, don't you know? Hell, I never had any reason to suspect a thing. Happened right before you came back from Panther Mountain, I imagine, Marshal Long. Went to scratchin' 'round to clean out your bay gelding's stall. Done found her all buried up under a pile of hay." Newman's head fell to his chest. Torturous, pained moans rose up in the man's withered chest. He pulled at his hair. "Good God, Almighty," he sobbed. "This cain't be real. Jest gotta be nothin' but a bad dream. Nightmare. Gotta wake up. Don't feel connected to my own body any longer."

Longarm pulled his pistol, checked each chamber, and placed a live round in the one he usually kept empty for safety's sake. He holstered the gun, stomped to Buster Byers's gun rack, pulled down a short-barreled shotgun and loaded it. He snapped the breech closed, turned to Hatchet and said, "Mica, being as how you're officially deputized already, I need you to stay here until I get back. Will you do that for me?"

Hatchett nodded. "Of course."

Longarm touched Marley Newman's father on the

shoulder. "Which stall, Mr. Newman? Which stall is she in?"

Without looking up, and in a barley audible rasp, Newman replied, "Third one on the right. Sure you cain't miss it. Only left the one gate open. Scared me so bad when I found her, sure I didn't close it."

Serious as death coming to breakfast, Longarm headed for the door and motioned for Pike to follow. "I'm going to depend on you to cover my back, Brax. Can you do that for me?"

Pike pulled a silver-plated, scroll-engraved, artillery model Colt's pistol and gave it a fancy spin on his finger. "Lead on, Marshal Long. You're as safe as a week-old babe, long as I'm alive and kickin'. Gua-ran-goddam-tee-it."

As he stepped across the threshold and onto the jail's little raised porch, Longarm called back over his shoulder, "Lock the damned door, Mica. Kill anyone, other than me or Brax, who might try to get in."

Chapter 18

Longarm and Braxton Pike darted across the wagon-rutted main thoroughfare to the entrance of an abandoned saddle maker's shop. The ghostly, deserted building's boarded windows stared blankly at the empty street and took little note of the grim-faced men who scampered onto its ill-used plank porch.

Backs against the wall, the men quickly worked their way along the raised boardwalk, past the entrance to Furlong's stable-fragrant hotel and rooming house and scurried up to the still-open doorway of Newman's livery barn.

"Stay by the door and watch the street, Brax," Longarm said. "I'll go in first and have a look."

"You got it, Marshal. Be careful."

One step at a time, with cocked weapon in hand, Longarm moved into the barn's aromatic gloom. He eased to the right side of the building, and moved past two closed stalls, until he reached the only one standing open in the entire stable.

Weblike shafts of bright sunlight knifed from numerous directions, sliced their way into the shadowy interior.

Thin, rolling clouds of ever-present dust particles danced upward along each beam.

Longarm's remount bay stood tied outside his usual spot and patiently waited for someone to move him to more comfortable surroundings. Walnut-sized horse flies buzzed about the animal's ankles and caused him to occasionally stamp his feet, flick his black tail, and shake his head. The animal's bridle jingled and clinked.

Longarm held the shotgun out at the ready, as he slipped around the open gate. He patted the horse on the neck, and crept into the pen's hay- and trash-littered interior. A disturbed area, in the farthest corner, sported a heaped-up mound of the used silage.

Behind the pile of hay and horse manure, Longarm found the partially clad body of Marley Newman—nude from the waist up. "Damnation," he whispered. An overpowering feeling of compassion, coupled with intense revulsion, hit the bottom of his stomach as he propped the shotgun against the wall and squatted over the corpse.

Unexpected movement behind him caused the now angry, agitated, and dismayed lawman to stand and twirl, drawn pistol in hand, only to confront the equally jumpy Braxton Pike.

"Dammit, Brax. Thought I told you to watch the door," Longarm snapped.

"You did at that, but the street's empty as last night's beer bottles, Long. Ain't nobody comin' this way. Hell, ain't even nobody in sight."

Pike watched as Longarm, with some degree of obvious reluctance, holstered the Frontier model Colt's pistol, and resumed his position beside the girl's crumpled body. "Well, as long as you're here, Brax, might as well help me turn her over. There's bruises on the sides of her neck that look like a man's finger marks. If we find some on the front, around her windpipe, I'll have to assume she was strangled."

With Pike at Marley Newman's feet, Longarm took the girl under the arms and rolled her onto her back.

"Sweet Jesus," Pike said as he recoiled, bolted away from the corpse, and turned his back. "I ain't seen nothin' like this since my days fightin' the Comanche when I wasn't much more'n a nubbin'."

"She's a dreadful sight for sure."

"Christ Almighty, Long, them look like bite marks all over her tits. Son of a bitch damned nigh bit that one nipple clean off. What the hell kind of animal does something so brutally heartless to a pretty girl like Marley?"

Longarm shook his head, then said, "The jealous kind, I think. Same kind that choked the life out of her after he'd done as he pleased. Her split skirt looks intact, but, in truth, it's ripped from hem to crotch. She's bruised up here all around her pubis as well. Blackened eye. Split lip. Some pretty rough sex going on before she died. Awful way to go out of this world, if you ask me, and even if you don't."

"God Almighty, but I do hate to see a woman mistreated like some kinda animal," Pike said as he averted his eyes and shook his head in disgust. "I mean, hell, admit as how I've done some pretty shitty things in my life. Ain't above gunning a man from behind, if'n he might be faster'n me and the opportunity to kill him 'fore he kills me arises. Low stuff. But, by God, I never done nothing this low. Christ, just how far down do you have to sink to abuse a woman in such a fashion?"

Longarm stood and let out a long, tired sigh. "Maybe she was already unconscious, on the way to being dead when he did all this. Leastways, those of us still living can hope so. Swear before Jesus, though, it simply doesn't matter how many times I've seen the pale, cold face of death in the past. Coming on the murder of a beautiful and passionate woman of my personal acquaintance still has the power to affect me in the most profound manner."

Pike ripped his hat off and slapped it against his leg. "What 'er we gonna do, goddammit? Jesse Burton needs to die in the worst kinda way for butchery like this. Tell you what, Long, if you don't kill the son of a bitch I sure as hell will."

While still staring at the brutalized body of Marley Newman, in a barely audible voice Longarm said, "Right now you're going to run down the street. Get Josh Smoot. Want you to explain the situation and tell him to bring his wagon." He touched Pike on the arm and locked eyes with the angry gunfighter. "But that's as far as I want the tale of what happened here to go, you hear me, Brax? Don't you dare inform anyone else about what we've found, until Smoot can make it over here, get her out, and properly cared for. Besides, I want this kept quiet until I can talk with Jesse Burton and those two idiots who work for him."

"Talk, hell. I think we should run the woman-murderin' bastard to ground, startin' right this very damned minute and, when we find him, kill the runny shit out of him—and them other scum suckers that cover his ass all the time, if they had any truck in this ugly mess."

"Don't trouble yourself on that account, Brax. He'll be dealt with. 'Fore God, I swear it. Now get on over to Smoot's and bring him here on the run."

As soon as Pike disappeared, Longarm rummaged around and found a blanket. He gazed into her face one last time, then carefully covered Marley Newman's pitiable, battered remains, stood and said, "Good God, girl, you had so much more to see. So much more to do. So many more people to meet." Then, the troubled marshal snatched up his shotgun, moved outside the stall, leaned heavily against the open gate, and lit himself a comforting cheroot.

Before Longarm could finish half his smoke, Panther Mountain's rail-thin, gloomy-faced undertaker appeared. He wore an immaculate, black, funereal outfit complete with stovepipe hat, starched white shirt with a new collar, and a freshly-cut day lily in the button hole of his swallow-tailed coat.

In a most professional and mournful tone, Smoot laced his fingers together, held them over his chest and said, "And where is the body of the dearly departed located, Marshal Long?"

Longarm pointed tiredly into the stall and said, "Far corner. She's only partially dressed, Josh. I looked, but couldn't find her blouse. Might be under some of the hay and stuff, I suppose."

"Mr. Pike told me as much as he could of what he'd seen, sir. I thought, given the girl's state of undress and such, it best to bring a female associate along with me."

Smoot moved to one side and motioned Serita to the scene of Marley Newman's vicious passing. The beautiful girl swept past them. Then, he placed a reassuring hand on Longarm's shoulder and said, "We'll take the best of care with Miss Newman, I assure you, Marshal." Longarm nodded absentmindedly, crushed the cigar under his heel, and made a beeline for the street.

A weeping Walker Newman flew by Longarm as he stepped out the stable's double door. He made a grab for the suffering stable owner's arm, but found it impossible to restrain Marley's grief-stricken father. Hell, if it was my daughter, Longarm thought, I'd want to be there by her side, too. No matter how awful the scene.

Pike was waiting in the street and trailed behind as the gloomy-faced marshal strode back to the jailhouse. He said, "What'er we gonna do, Long? Look on your face tells me you've come to some kind of decision, like you've got something in mind. Personally hope it involves killin' the hell out of Jesse Burton. Want to let me in on your plans?"

Custis Long hit the Panther Mountain jail's front door so hard Mica Hatchett almost jumped out of his skin. "Damnation, man," Hatchett yelped, as he waved the cocked shotgun around. "Came near poppin' a cap on your careless ass. You oughta have at least a pound's more sense than to bust in here on me like that. Hell, situation's wound up tighter'n a eight-day clock and you're runnin' around like a chicken with its head wrung off. Shit almighty! Kind of behavior could get a man killed deader'n a can of corned beef."

"Sorry, Mica, just wasn't thinking straight," Longarm said. He marched to Buster Byers's gun rack, jerked a second shotgun down, loaded and handed it to Braxton Pike. He filled his pockets with shells, then checked his own weapon. "You boys still want to gut up, load up, and confront the Moon bunch?"

"Damn straight," Pike snapped back.

"Am I to take it you boys found the girl exactly as her father described?" Hatchett asked.

Longarm stared at the floor. "Yes, she's dead alright. It was a brutal killing, Mica. One of the worst I've ever seen."

"Me, too," Pike added.

"Then I guess the best thing, all the way around, is to

hoof it down to the Red Onion. See if we can corral Jesse Burton and the Tubbs brothers. Far as I'm concerned, if the Moon boys get their backs up, we might as well take care of them, too," Hatchett said.

"Good to hear we're all singing from the same hymn book," Longarm said and heeled it for the street. "'Cause we're gonna stroll down to the Onion, see if anyone knows how to find Jesse Burton. If the Moon bunch tries to interfere, or causes us one second's worth of trouble, well, far as I'm concerned, they're as good as dead meat. We'll march down together, rush in before anyone has a chance to realize what's up, and if a single man there touches his weapon, we'll blast the hell out of all of them."

Chapter 19

Longarm and his shotgun-carrying companions stalked down the street, lined up side by side. They quickly covered the eerily empty hundred yards of dusty, rutted roadway to the Red Onion and stepped onto the saloon's pillared porch armed to the teeth and itching for a fight.

With a single furtive glance, Longarm took silent note of the smoldering flames of gun smoke and death flickering behind Pike's and Hatchett's slitted eyes. Tight-lipped, he nodded in each man's direction, and then pushed his way through the Onion's batwing doors.

Once inside, Pike slipped to the bar on Longarm's left and covered two surprised gunmen standing about midway down. The wide-eyed pistoleers froze in shocked amazement. Drinks, held in trembling hands, hovered at their lips. Bartender Everett Turner moved away from his customers. He edged a few steps along the back bar and nervously glanced around in search of the nearest safe spot.

Mica Hatchett went to Longarm's right, slid along the wall, and stopped in the corner. He winked, nodded his readiness, and aimed the ever-present, ghostly, gold-plated blaster at a group of wide-eyed gamblers that loafed at the felt-covered table located farthest from the batwing doors.

Longarm brought his .10-gauge scattergun to bear on the same table. The three Moon boys took on the frozen aspect of marble statues. They gaped at the bold intruders in disbelief. A fourth man that Longarm took as Clyde Stillwell sat with the Moon clan amidst piles of whiskey bottles and playing cards, stacks of chips, mounds of loose currency or coin, and a dense cloud of tobacco smoke.

Alarmed by the unexpected entrance of a steely-eyed, heavily armed group, all the local gamblers, tipplers, and scarlet women hit their feet, scattered, and heeled it for the most accessible exit, or the best available shelter that could be obtained.

Longarm brazenly marched up to within a few feet of the Moon gang's fun. Everyone at the table appeared to blanch. From the corner of his eye, he saw whiskey-slinger Everett Turner toss his towel aside and scamper to a sheltered nook at the far end of his carefully polished counter. The nervous barkeep glanced from Hatchett to Longarm to Pike and back again, before burrowing into the niche like a man convinced that clouds of death-dealing lead would soon fill the air.

Longarm's attention flicked back to the Moon bunch. With a deliberate motion, he waved the shotgun from one man at the table to the next. Finally he growled, "I want that little son of a bitch, Jesse Burton, and I want him right by God now."

A bleary-eyed, whiskey-faced, bulbous-nosed man who looked distinctly like Hangtown Harry Moon's shorter, skinnier, uglier twin, leaned his chair back on two legs. He ceremoniously hooked his thumbs over a concho-decorated pistol belt and snarled, "Just who in the blue-eyed hell's a-askin', if'n I might be so bold as to inquire?"

Longarm grimaced. Fought back the urge to splatter the smart-mouthed drunk all over Hell and yonder. "Deputy United States Marshal Custis Long's asking. Which one of the Moon clan are you?" he shot back.

"My name's Shooter, by God. And what the hell's it to you, you nosey son of a bitch? You writin' some kinda goddamned book or somethin'? Gotta lotta nerve stormin' up to our table, a-brandishin' weapons, and a-makin' demands, you mouthy bastard. We don't even know who you are." His words came out slurred by the nearly day-long consumption of bottled courage.

Stump Moon scraped the steel-tipped end of his wooden leg across the floor, as he turned slightly toward Longarm. The one-legged, scar-faced, odiferous pile of rags, who sat next to Hangtown Harry's mouthy brother Shooter, drunkenly placed a half full tumbler of Old Panther Juice on the table and said, "My, oh, my. Done got right tense around here at the Red Onion, ain't it boys? Think you should go on and careful-up there, Shooter. Pert sure you wouldn't want to piss this here feller off, now would you?"

"Son of a bitch can go straight to a flame-kissed hell, far as I'm concerned," Shooter snorted.

"Let's be cautious now brother," Stump said. "Think this here situation is exactly like our dear ole, sainted, white-haired Mama always said, you should never piss a feller off what's got the drop on you with a sawed-off shotgun."

Shooter Moon let his chair thump back to the floor, and went to scratching a spot over his ear. "Hell, I don't remember Ma ever sayin' nothin' like that, Stump. When did she say that? Near as I can remember all the hateful old bitch ever done was quote the Bible at me just 'fore beatin' hell out of me for one of her ten thousand pet transgressions or 'nother."

"Well, I could be wrong about my memory of the thing bein' Ma a-warnin' us. Maybe that particular admonition can only be found in the Good Book somewheres. Guess I mighta heard it read out from Leviticus, Numbers, Deuteronomy, or Psalms whilst I was attending Sunday school at the church, one time or 'tother, back when we was all kids in Alabama. Could be, I'm just re-memberin' a lesson from one of them hellfire and brimstone books, you know. Not exactly sure which. All the nose paint we've consumed today mighta done affected my memory. She ain't in the New Testament though, what with all that peace, love your neighbor, and do good to your fellow man bullshit. Know for damned certain it didn't come from there."

Shooter Moon hocked up a pecan-sized wad of phlegm, spat on the floor, then turned back to Longarm. "The hell with 'im and all the other nervy sons of bitches like 'im, Stump. Can't believe these three dumb bastards done got up the outright audacity to brace the Moon gang whilst they's all a-recreatin', relaxin', lettin' off steam and such. Not botherin' a soul, by God."

Snaggle-toothed, rail-thin, and sallow-faced, Stillwell, the odd man in the group, who sat closest to where Longarm stood, said, "Now, wait a minute here, fellers. I think that perhaps, since we've got us none other than Deputy United States Marshal Custis Long, we should be on our best behavior. Hell, he's the gent what's a-holding Hangtown Harry down to the jail. Ain't that the true case of the matter, Marshal?"

Longarm shook his head, then said, "Hangtown

Harry's got no part in why I'm here today, Stillwell. I came to arrest Jesse Burton for murder and, for the second time, I want him right by God now. So, either give him up, or get a case of the smarts, for the first time in your benighted lives, and tell me where the murderous weasel is."

"We don't know where the little weasel is," offered the only Moon brother left who hadn't spoken.

"Ah, hell, Axel," Shooter Moon snorted, "don't be tellin' this walkin' stack of badge-wearin' skunk shit anything 'cept maybe to kiss your saddle-widened, hairy ass. Us Moon boys don't owe him a damned thang. Besides, he ain't even said why he's a-lookin' for Burton yet."

Clyde Stillwell's skeletal face broke into an arrogant grin. A hacking laugh coughed its way to his cracked lips. "Yeah, Axel, don't tell the badge-totin' bastard nothin'. He's gotta lotta damned nerve comin' in here a-callin' us be-nighted, by God. Be-nighted for Christ's sake. Ain't nobody ever had nerve enough to call me be-nighted to my face a-fore in my entire life. Why, he's the same badge-totin' son of a bitch what kilt our good friend and *amigo bueno* Willy Coffin."

Axel Moon waved at Stillwell. "Give it a rest, Clyde. Ain't no point in pissin' this feller off any worse than he already is."

Stillwell snorted, "Aw, hell, Axel, I'll vow he ain't got balls enough to march right up here in the middle of men as bad as us and actually do anything . . ."

Before Stillwell could finish his ill-conceived, smart-assed remarks, Longarm took two giant steps toward the table, brought the shotgun's butt around, and smacked Stillwell flat in the face. Several rotten, yellow-stained teeth flew out both sides of the astonished bad man's mouth.

Stillwell's winged teeth, accompanied by a fist-sized gout of blood, sprayed in every direction: hit the pile of discarded cardboards, ricocheted and splashed molars, and blood all over the shirtfronts of Shooter and Stump Moon, who had their chairs pulled up closest to the famed Texas gunfighter.

Another smack and a sickening, rotten, twiglike crunch of breaking cartilage in Stillwell's hooked, flattened nose resounded from wall to wall in the now-quiet room. Almost instantly, a geyser of reddish-purple gore spewed across the table from his fractured proboscis, in a near fire hose–like squirt every time his heart beat. The flabbergasted gunman let out a girly-sounding screech, grabbed at his demolished face, flopped onto the floor like a beached fish, and rolled around in his own spurting blood.

An incensed Stump Moon awkwardly clambered to his only remaining foot and slapped at the sticky mess decorating his vest. Bug-eyed, slobbering like a hydrophobic dog, he held a gore-speckled hand out at Longarm and screeched, "Damn you to an eternal hell, you son of a bitch. You had no call to do that. Clyde was just running off at the mouth. Didn't mean nothin'. Besides, I just bought this here suit coat and vest last week, now look at it." Then, he pushed the tail of his woolen jacket back and made threatening moves for the Remington pistol strapped high on his right hip.

Longarm brought the shotgun around to cover the apparent threat and said, "Even a one-legged, half-brained, chicken-gutted idiot like you can't be stupid enough to pull a pistol on a man who'll kill you deader than a rotten telegraph pole, Stump."

Stuck with his fingers twitching above the grips of the Remington, Moon's chapped lips quivered when he snarled, "'Fore this day is out, swear to Jesus, I'm gonna kill you, Marshal Custis by God Long."

Brother Axel, hands prominently displayed on the green felt tabletop with fingers spread, said through gritted teeth, "Calm down, Stump. They's plenty of time to kill this long, tall, stack of walking steer manure. Hell, we've got all the time in the world. Don't do him today, we can do him tomorrow."

Stump's lips stretched thin over tobacco-stained teeth as he slobbered, "I want him now, brother. Want him dead, right here at my feet. Once we've kilt him, I'm gonna rip off his head and skull fuck 'im in the eyehole just for the sheer mean-assed Moon brother's fun of it."

Without looking in the barman's direction, Longarm shouted, "Everett, has Jesse been in here today?"

From down low, out of sight behind the bar, Everett Turner croaked, "Early this mornin'. Ain't seen him since. From what I've been able to hear, the Moon brothers are tellin' you the truth, Marshal. They ain't seen him either, not in here anyways."

Longarm lowered his shotgun ever so slightly. "Well, you boys don't have any idea how lucky you are today. Damned good thing you're not hiding the woman-killing bastard."

Stump Moon actually looked shocked. "Woman killer? What the hell are you talking about, Marshal? Ain't none of us know a damned thing about no woman killing."

Every man left in the room perked up, turned an attentive ear toward Longarm. "We just uncovered the corpse of Walker Newman's daughter, Marley. Found her buried under a pile of hay down at the livery. Way we've got it figured right now, Jesse Burton was the last man seen with the girl, and most likely the man responsible for her untimely demise."

A red-faced Stump Moon shook his finger at Long-arm. "Us Moon boys got no truck with woman-killers. Jesse Burton comes back in here, we'll snatch him up. Personally turn him over to you ourselves."

Longarm almost laughed out loud at such a prospect, but held it in and said, "Doubt you'll get the chance to snatch anyone up, Stump, because here's the other part of the reason I'm here today. My friends and I are going to make our way out into the street and head back to the mar-shal's office. That'll give you boys a chance to see to the care and comfort of your friend, Stillwell, and get your-selves back together. Then, you've got exactly one hour to sober up, saddle up, and get the hell out of Panther Moun-tain. If you choose not to leave, we'll come back—and we'll come back blasting."

Axel and Shooter Moon jumped to wobbly feet and threw coattails away from their pistols. Shooter yelped, "Well, by God, you can fold that smart-mouthed order five ways and stick it where the sun don't shine, you arro-gant cocksucker. Ain't no man alive tells the Moon boys where they can, or cain't go or stay."

Calm as the bottom of a freshly dug post hole, Long-arm backed his way toward the batwing doors, stopped at the entrance and said, "Any man touches a weapon, and we'll send all three of you dumb sons of bitches to hell on an outhouse door."

Outside in the street, and on their way back to the jail, Hatchett and Pike kept glancing back over their shoul-ders. Pike said, "Why didn't we just go on ahead and kill 'em all? Thought that was the whole reason why we came stormin' down here in the first place. Ain't a good idea to let men like the Moon boys off the hook, once you've got 'em strung up."

Without warning, barely a dozen or so steps away

170

from the Red Onion's entrance, a fusillade of pistol shots chewed holes in the air all around Longarm and his companions like angry Mexican hornets. One punched through the crown of Longarm's hat, knocked it off his head, and plowed a burning, but far from mortal, crease in his hair. Another sizzled through his vest and shirt, then scorched a smoking trench along the flesh of his right side. All three men twirled and, at almost the same instant, unleashed a lethal barrage of return fire from their shotguns.

A torrent of hot lead sprayed the Onion's front façade. Flanked by their toadies, Stump, Axel, and Shooter Moon caught the death-dealing brunt of six barrels of heavy-gauge buckshot. Hundreds of murderous metal pellets shattered the Onion's etched, plate-glass window. Others peppered and notched every wooden surface, blasted the batwing doors to splinters, even wounded two men at the very edges of the action. Blood, rendered cloth, and bits of flesh painted the thick Texas air in a reddish, purple spray. One man somehow managed to remain standing under the onslaught.

The roar and concussion set Longarm's ears to ringing like cathedral bells. A dense, rolling, metallic-colored cloud of spent black powder made it difficult, but not impossible, to see much. It eventually became clear to the wounded lawman that three, or four, maybe five gunnies, who had lined up on the saloon's front porch, now lay wounded, dead, or dying from the blistering hailstorm of flesh-riddling lead that he, Hatchett, and Pike had unleashed.

Longarm pitched the .10-gauge shoulder cannon aside, drew his Colt pistol, and took careful, two-handed aim at the only man he could see moving amidst the dense curtain of acrid-tasting, eye-burning gun smoke.

He recognized the wounded gun hand as one of those Pike had covered at the bar. The man stumbled from the boardwalk and lurched into the street. Smoke from searing buckshot balls leaked from near a dozen places in the man's jacket, pants, and face. His right arm dangled limply inside a bloodied, rendered sleeve, and he'd shifted a long-barreled cavalry model Colt pistol to his off hand.

"I'm gonna kill the hell out of you, bastards," the wounded man screeched. He awkwardly raised the pistol and fired a shot that hit the ground at Longarm's feet, ricocheted off a spot between his legs, whistled away, and struck a horse tied at the hitch rack in front of Harlan's Grocery. The animal screeched, dropped like a felled tree, and ran in place as though trying to get away from the pain.

A single report from Longarm's pistol delivered a 255-grain .45-caliber slug into the swaying gunman's skull, just under his right eye. The huge chunk of metal exited at the base of his skull in a massive wad of bone, brain matter, and blood. Wide-eyed and unblinking, the surprised *pistolero* rocked back on his heels, hung in the air like a puppet suspended on invisible strings, then collapsed in a gore-saturated, ragged heap.

Mica Hatchett said, "Damn, that was blisterin' stuff."

Longarm spat to clear his mouth of the coppery taste of blood hanging in the air, then turned to see Billy Vail's old friend, on his knees, in the dusty street. A hole in the man's chest gushed life in a scarlet flood from between fingers pressed over the gaping wound. Braxton Pike knelt beside the old Ranger and tried, at first, to keep the wounded man upright. Longarm dropped to one knee and helped Pike lay Hatchett out on his back.

As they propped their wounded friend's head on his

hat, Hatchett limply grabbed at Longarm's hand and gasped, "Got me in that . . . first volley. Surprised the belly-slinkin' snakes had the nerve. Didn't . . . even feel the slug . . . go through. Not at first, anyway."

With a powder-stained bare hand, Longarm wiped thumb-sized beads of sweat from Hatchett's forehead. "Well, in that case, maybe it didn't hit anything important, Mica. Sounds like there's a good chance we can . . ."

"No. No, young . . . feller. I'm done. Shit . . . never expected to go out like this. Thought my fightin' days . . . was over till you . . . showed up."

"Aw, hell, Mica, I've seen men shot a lot worse what pulled through," Pike offered through a shaky grin.

Hatchett's eyes closed, then opened only halfway. "Don't trouble yerselves, boys. Angel of death's . . . been after me . . . for most'a my life. Do me a favor, Long. Say good-bye . . . to Billy Vail. My shotgun . . . give it to him. He always admired the damned thing. Rather . . . he had it than . . ."

Longarm leaned over and placed his ear next to the fallen man's mouth. He sat up, wagged his head like a tired dog, and said, "Sweet Jesus, that happened quick, Brax. Can't believe he's gone. Ole bony-fingered death snatched the life out of him so fast he couldn't even finish his sentence. Damn."

As Longarm and Pike came to their feet again, Josh Smoot and his solemn-faced assistant ran up pulling their squeaky two-wheeled body wagon. "We've got one hell of a mess to clean up here, Josh," Longarm said.

"Yes, indeed, Marshal. Indeed, we do."

Before Longarm, Pike, and Smoot could completely tally the day's total cost in dead men, Buster Byers rode up and climbed off his horse. He stumbled onto the Onion's short piece of shot-peppered, blood-drenched boardwalk, snatched off his sweat-stained hat, then said, "Damnation, Marshal Long, ain't seen carnage like this since fightin' at Pea Ridge durin' the Great War of Yankee Aggression. Sweet Jesus, never thought, for a single instant, a little thing like me lockin' ole Hangtown Harry up would come to a kill-off like this."

Longarm stood in a puddle of coagulating gore that almost came over the soles of his boots and gazed down at Stump, Axel, and Shooter Moon's oozing corpses. He shook his head, then glared at Byers and said, "Well, Buster, just what in hell did you think would happen? Must have had some idea. Your rather protracted absence, over the past few days, would lead just about any thinking man to believe you feared events might develop that were very much along the lines of what actually transpired."

"Honestly, sir, never, in my wildest imaginings, did it occur to me that anything approaching six dead men on the streets of my town at one time would take place. 'Fore God, I swear it."

Longarm shook his head in disgust. "Yeah. Well, you've also got a dead woman to deal with, too."

Somehow Josh Smoot, and a multitude of Mexican coffin makers, once again, worked miracles for Marshal Custis Long. By late the following afternoon, a hastily arranged mass burial, of most of the Moon gang, took place in Panther Mountain's tiny Cottonwood Cemetery. Braxton Pike called the event "the great plantin'."

Almost everyone who still lived in town attended the burial, in spite of the fact that none of them knew the dead men, or actually even cared that they'd met their Maker in such a violent manner. Longarm even cuffed Hangtown Harry and saw to it the shattered outlaw attended the ceremony that commemorated the passing of his three brothers.

As Everett Turner said, "Just seemed like the right and proper thing to do when folks pass on to the Great Beyond. Somebody ought to see 'em off, no matter what kind of skunk they were in this life. And besides, makes for great conversation over a drink down at the saloon when the thing's all said and done. But you know, personally, I think most folks just wanted to make sure the sons of bitches were completely, by God, dead and covered over with a nice pile of freshly dug earth."

A day later, a far more solemn event marked the sad interment of Marley Newman and Mica Hatchett. Longarm stood beside Walker Newman during the services. Spent most of his time trying to hold the grief-stricken man erect.

Afterward, over a glass of Maryland rye with Braxton Pike, Longarm said, "I've attended more than my share of services over the years, but can't bring to mind a single time that I've ever been more profoundly affected than I was this afternoon. Especially liked that part when Josh Smoot likened Marley and Mica's passing to a trip on a ship, and how we'd all have to sail away from this vale of tears on the same boat someday. It's been a deadly and difficult couple of days, very difficult, and I think his words offered considerable comfort for everyone, especially Marley's father. Leastways I certainly hope so."

The morning after Marley and Mica's sad memorials, the only remaining member of the Moon family dejectedly mounted a rented horse. In front of Newman's Livery, he waited in tight-lipped silence as Longarm readied everything for the bleak fifty-mile trip back to Fort Stockton and transport to Denver. Joshua Smoot stood by and watched.

"Don't want to wait around for any more of the Moon clan to show up. Tell Mr. Newman I'll leave his animal at the remount station, Josh. He can pick it up at his leisure. I'll see he's paid his regular rate until he can come after the beast," Longarm said and pulled the cinch tight on the bay gelding.

He stepped into the metal stirrup, hoisted himself aboard, and settled onto the McClellan. "Make sure Buster follows up on Marley Newman's murder," he added. "Jesse Burton needs hanging, and that happy event can't come soon enough to suit me. I've also told him to hold One-Eyed Charlie and Whitey for another day, or two, before he turns them loose. Wouldn't want to have those boys catch me out on the trail between here and Fort Stockton and lay an ambush."

Smoot patted the gelding's neck, then said, "I'll do my level best to make sure Buster does as you've told him, Marshal Long. You have my word on the matter. But, as you've already discovered, man's something of an empty vessel. Don't pay to expect much from him."

Longarm leaned down and offered his hand. As he and Smoot shook, he said, "Might not get back this way before Panther Mountain's nothing more than a fleeting memory, Josh. Hope the best for you and yours, sir."

Within a matter of minutes, Longarm and his murderous prisoner had disappeared in a cloud of blowing sand. Nothing more than fading memories.

Chapter 20

Longarm sat next to Hangtown Harry Moon on a rock hard bench at Fort Stockton's virtually deserted depot and rummaged through his possibles bag, while they waited for the next train north to El Paso. He pulled out a fistful of nickel cheroots and stuffed them into various vest pockets. Then lit one for himself and one for his prisoner. Their smokes were barely half gone when movement off to the right flickered across the corner of his eye.

Someone said, "I've come to kill you. Get on yer feet, you lanky son of a bitch."

Moon whispered, "Hope he pulls it off, Long. Hope he kills you deader'n a rotten tree stump."

Longarm stood, resettled the pistol belt around his waist, glanced at his belligerent adversary, then said, "Would have bet my McClellan saddle that you'd skipped the country, Jesse. Where are the idiot Tubbs brothers these days?"

Barely fifteen feet down the loading platform, Jesse Burton licked his lips like a beady-eyed, coiled up rattlesnake and sneered. "Them two chicken shits ain't got guts enough to take part in my plans. Told 'em it was time you paid fer what happened to Marley, but the weak-kneed lily-livers skinned out on me. Bettin' man would say they's probably down in Mexico suckin' up *cerveza*. Likely they's a-wallerin' with Messican whores, by now."

"Think your memory of past events has got turned on its head, don't you, Jesse? I didn't have anything to do with Marley Newman's brutal and untimely death."

Burton's face reddened. "The hell you say. Everthang 'twixt me and Marley wuz a-goin' along just fine and dandy till you went and showed up, you slick-talkin' son of a bitch. Poor ole country boy like me cain't compete with fellers what show up in places like Panther Mountain an' work their worldly ways on raw young women like my Marley."

"That's a damned sorry excuse for what you did, Jesse."

"Hell, I never woulda lost my temper the way I done, if'n it hadn't been for her tellin' me all about how the two of you done the nasty on Panther Mountain's jailhouse floor." Burton got louder and he shook his finger at Longarm. "Gal called me a tiny-dicked son of a bitch, right to my face, for Christ's sake. Said you was gonna take her back to Denver. Said I could go straight to hell. Damn you, Long. Damn you for stealin' her away from me."

"Calm down, Jesse. Believe me when I tell you, that whatever Marley said to you was probably done in unthinking anger and, trust me when I say, you don't want this dance to go any farther than it already has."

"Well, fuck you, and the hammerheaded cayuse you rode from Panther Mountain, Long. 'Cause the time's done come for you to die."

Burton's hand darted for the pistol on his hip. Four thunderous shots delivered .45-caliber slugs that drilled a like number of holes in his chest before he even had a chance to clear leather. Shocked and surprised, the dying woman-killer grabbed at the gushing wounds. Somehow, he managed to get his weapon out, and fire off one wild shot a split-second before he hit his knees, then tumbled blindly onto his face, and death came to blow out the flickering candle in his feeble brain.

Longarm turned and glanced over at Hangtown Harry Moon. The outlaw's head lolled onto one shoulder. Jesse Burton's stray round had hit the lawdog's prisoner in the jaw and come out his right eye. On its way to parts unknown, the huge slug had splattered a gob of teeth, bone, eyeball, and brain matter all over the unfortunate man's lap. He still held a burning cheroot between his now dead fingers.

Standing over the outlaw's corpse, Longarm shook his head and gazed down at the various holes in Hangtown Harry Moon's shattered noggin. "Been one hell of a bad week for you, hasn't it, Harry?" he said. "Personally, right at this very moment, I can't imagine how it could have been any worse. But I'll give it some thought on the ride back to Denver." He slipped the Frontier model Colt back into its holster.

"Shit," he mumbled to himself, "now I've got to make arrangements for you two bastards to get buried. Getting mighty tired of funerals, but, by God, I am not sticking around for these particular doings. But first, guess maybe I'd best let Billy Vail know what's gone and transpired here. Bet he ain't gonna like the news, but there's nothing I can do about it now." With that, he turned on his heel and headed for the stationmaster's office.

Matilda Potter didn't bother to knock. A copper-colored sun dropped behind the Rockies snow-covered peaks, as she slipped into Longarm's barely lit, disheveled room.

She quietly closed the door and leaned against the wall. His totally naked, brawny form on the bed stoked the glowing fire between her legs and forced raging flames upward to breasts that ached with desire. An insistent hand crept inside her blouse and caressed an already aroused nipple to finger-hard stiffness.

Longarm sat up, fluffed his pillow, and said, "I like the hat, Tildy. Got a real nice Texas brush popper's crimp on it. You bring your riding crop along, too, girl? Seems as how I remember you saying you might."

A brilliant, mischievous smile flashed across her face. "No, but I wore my ridin' spurs." In an instant, the girl's skirt laces were loosed, and the garment fell to her booted feet in a crumpled heap. She slid a hand down to her ebony thatch and caressed herself.

"Why, Tildy, that's so very lewd. You're not wearin' any underthings, girl. Can't believe you walked all the way over here in such a state of undress. If I didn't know better, I'd think you planned to seduce me."

She threw her head back, leaned against the wall, closed her eyes, moaned, and said, "Well, I rushed over as soon as I got your note. Why waste time gettin' dressed, bein' as how you're here and gone so often. Besides, I like the way it feels when I walk down the street as close to nekkid as I can get." She kicked the skirt under the bed, stripped her blouse off, dropped it on the floor, and sent it flying to a spot beside the skirt. Solid silver Mexican rowels jingled and sang as she strode majestically to Longarm's bedside. She stopped, leaned over, and raked her fingers along the inside of his thigh.

"Damn girl, your hand feels like it's on fire," he said, as she toyed with his hardening manhood. She stroked his balls, then bent over, and licked him into a state of near frenzy. He pushed the hat off her head, slid his fingers

180

into silken, ebony tresses and urged her lips over his now rigid, throbbing tool.

After several minutes of the girl's concentrated efforts, he grabbed at her hair again, but missed as she moved away. "God, I do like the way you taste, Custis," she said, "but I've got other things in mind right now."

She threw a leg over his waiting body and straddled his raging prong. Hands locked to the brass bedstead, she slid herself onto him, and bounced to the rhythm of the powerfully built form that bucked and humped beneath her.

Ten minutes into a tooth-rattling ride, she squealed, "Oh, sweet Lord above."

Longarm grabbed her hips and jammed himself deeper into her heavenly, moist center. "Damn, Tildy, you're not sitting on one of those spurs are you?"

The lusty girl pitched forward and fused overheated, sweat-drenched, stiff-nippled breasts to Longarm's chest. Her tongue filled his mouth, flicked around to his ear, traced a scorching path down his neck, then stopped and sucked a nipple till he came nigh to bucking her off into the floor.

Aroused almost beyond endurance, Longarm grunted, ran his hands up her back and pulled the girl forward. Her lush breasts brushed against his forehead. He raised his head and sucked one nipple, then the other, back and forth as fast as he could until she squealed again, then pulled herself away from his greedy mouth.

Before she could recover, Longarm flipped the compliant girl onto her back, her knees touching her breasts, spurs jingling like cathedral bells. His sweat-drenched body slapped loud and wet against hers.

Carefully manicured fingernails bit into his biceps. "Not yet! Not yet! Hang on, darlin'," she wailed. "Don't stop! Please!"

Time melted and ran through Longarm like heated syrup. His muscles bunched. He arched his back and tightened his buttocks—drew on his famed self-control to keep the inevitable from happening. The girl wiggled below him, then pulled herself up, tongued his ear, and whispered, "Now, darlin'! Now!" Then her free hand darted between them, and she caressed them both to a mutual, shuddering, molten climax.

For as long as he could, Longarm held the pose of rigid, ecstatic orgasm. Eventually, overstressed muscles could no longer maintain the posture, and he rolled to one side. Tildy snuggled up against his side and, as was her custom, soon feel into a deep, satisfied, sound sleep.

Warm, comfortable and sated, at least for the moment, Longarm pulled the beautiful Tildy closer and drifted off himself. Within minutes a hot, prickly sensation along his spine caused him to sit bolt upright and, for the most fleeting of moments, he would have sworn he saw Marley Newman standing at the foot of his bed.

Tildy stirred in his arms and mumbled, "Bad dream, darlin'?"

Longarm smiled. "No, Tildy. A very pleasant memory, actually."

Watch for

**LONGARM AND THE
SABOTAGED RAILROAD**

the 338th novel in the exciting LONGARM
series from Jove

Coming in January!

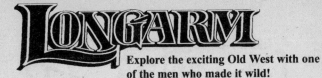

Explore the exciting Old West with one of the men who made it wild!

GIANT ACTION! GIANT ADVENTURE!

THE GUNSMITH

GIANT

Giant Westerns featuring The Gunsmith

**Little Sureshot and the
Wild West Show**
0-515-13851-7

Dead Weight
0-515-14028-7

Available in October 2006:
Red Mountain
0-515-14206-9

**Available wherever books are sold or at
penguin.com**

J799

LONGARM

GIANT-SIZED ADVENTURE FROM AVENGING ANGEL LONGARM.

COMING ↓ IN ↓ NOVEMBER 2006...

LONGARM AND THE OUTLAW EMPRESS
0-515-14235-2

WHEN DEPUTY U.S. MARSHAL CUSTIS LONG STOPS A STAGECOACH ROBBERY, HE TRACKS THE BANDITS TO A TOWN CALLED ZAMORA. A HAVEN FOR THE LAWLESS, IT'S RULED BY ONE OF THE MOST ⊠POWERFUL, BRILLIANT, AND BEAUTIFUL WOMEN IN THE WEST...A WOMAN WHOM LONGARM WILL HAVE TO FACE, UP CLOSE AND PERSONAL.